BRIDAL SALON

Full-Service Bridal Salon. Includes full stock of off-the-rack and made-to-order designer wedding gowns, headpieces, shoes and accessories. Also available: invitation books and florist and orchestra tie-ins, as well as studio apartment—perfect for single person—above the shop.

Reason for Sale: Current owner is about to become her own best customer!

Dear Reader,

Ah, yes...weddings. Reunions. Office parties. All those events that are just made for couples, people who walk in two by two, holding hands, smiling into each other's eyes... You get the picture. But for those of us who are not only single but currently unattached, it's more like being the center of attention for all the wrong reasons. "What's *she* doing here all alone? What a shame she hasn't got a boyfriend." Of course, maybe it's not a shame at all. Maybe "she" just decided to stop kissing frogs and let the handsome prince come looking for her. But still, it might be nice to have company on those occasions, and that's where Samantha Carter's *The Emergency Stand-By Date* comes in. It provides a novel solution to the dilemma, not to mention a happy—if unexpected—ending for the couple in question.

And then there's *Wedding Daze,* a first novel from brand-new author Karen Templeton. She used to work in a bridal salon herself, so she knows her background firsthand. Meet Brianna Fairchild and discover how it feels to spend your days planning everyone else's fantasy weddings, with no hint of your own groom in sight. Until you meet Spencer Lockhart, a confirmed bachelor with "Mr. Right" written all over him. Now, how to get him making a few wedding plans of his own...?

Have fun, and don't forget to come back next month for two more wonderful books all about unexpectedly meeting—and marrying!—Mr. Right.

Yours,

[signature]

Leslie Wainger
Senior Editor and Editorial Coordinator

Please address questions and book requests to:
Silhouette Reader Service
U.S.: 3010 Walden Ave., P.O. Box 1325, Buffalo, NY 14269
Canadian: P.O. Box 609, Fort Erie, Ont. L2A 5X3

KAREN TEMPLETON

Wedding Daze

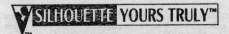

Published by Silhouette Books

America's Publisher of Contemporary Romance

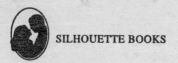

SILHOUETTE BOOKS

ISBN 0-373-52064-6

WEDDING DAZE

Printed in U.S.A.

Dear Reader,

One of the perks of being an associate buyer in a bridal salon is being able to try on scads of wedding gowns. By the time my husband finally got around to asking me to marry him, I had planned my wedding at least a dozen times over. Problem was, after five years of dragging his feet, he suddenly decided we should get married when his folks would be in town anyway—which gave us (read, ME) less than six weeks to pull together a formal wedding! For those six weeks, I was indeed in a total daze. The invitations had to be ordered before the chapel was confirmed; my gown wasn't ready until the day before the wedding (and came out stark white instead of the pale ivory I'd ordered); the flowers—and my maid of honor—showed up at the church less than twenty minutes before the service. I was a wreck. And happier than I'd ever been in my life.

Nineteen wonderful years and five sons later, I often think about things I might have changed about my wedding (if I'd had a minute to think about it). But the one thing I wouldn't change for all the money in the world is the groom, or the great kids we're raising together. Like Brianna discovers in *Wedding Daze*, bliss can come out of chaos!

Karen Templeton

1

———◄———

Spencer Lockhart lowered his briefcase to the floor in front of the unmanned—or, in this case, most likely *unwomanned*—reception desk, trying to maintain a neutral expression as he surveyed the ghastly decor of the waiting room. From floor to ceiling, the entire room was decorated in Pepto-Bismolian pink, a hue he'd always associated with nasty little girls and nosy old ladies.

He crammed his hands into the pockets of his camel hair topcoat, inwardly wincing as a shrill giggle assaulted his eardrums. Judging from the furtive glances and titters aimed in his direction, he had unwittingly caught the collective eye of a dozen or so bridesmaids.

Oh, yeah, he thought. Kelly would owe him *big* for this.

He checked his watch and frowned. Two forty-six. His appointment had been for two. Traffic had been even worse than he'd feared, and then he'd gotten lost on the twisted side streets of Inman Park trying to find the place. He stepped around the desk and peered down a hallway.

"Hello?"

There was no response, nothing save his own voice reverberating through the narrow passage, and some muffled conversation in the distance.

Annoyed, he returned to the reception desk, glowering at the still-ogling girls who immediately turned back into themselves like morning glories in late afternoon. Not sure what to do, Spencer sank into an overstuffed armchair upholstered in a hideous print fabric boasting roses the size of basketballs.

Another young thing sauntered through the front door.

"*Brandi!* Over here!"

Shrieking in response to her name, the girl named Brandi flew into the arms of the group as if she were Miss Georgia joining the group of semifinalists in the Miss America pageant, her left hand thrust out in front of her. The decibel level in the room escalated to dangerous levels as the girls gasped and clasped hands to bosoms and intermittently screamed "Oh, my *God!*" at what Spencer assumed was a recently acquired engagement ring.

No sooner had the flock settled down than they went into a frenzy again at the appearance of a wiry-haired older woman whose arms overflowed with filmy dresses in an array of vomit-inducing colors. As the girls descended on the poor woman like a bunch of squawking chickens at feeding time, he idly wondered if anyone, *anyone,* would ever be caught dead in that shade of fuchsia.

"Oh! I'm sorry! Are you being helped?"

Startled, Spencer shifted toward the slightly breathy female voice, accented with the modified drawl of a Southerner schooled north of the Mason-Dixon line. A tall, fashionably dressed woman with huge hazel eyes and a warm smile stood in front of him, clutching some folders to her chest.

The atmosphere had just improved considerably.

"Not yet." He stood. "Actually, I had an appointment for two, but I got stuck in traffic. The name's Lockhart. I trust you'll be able to fit me in."

"Oh, dear...I'm not sure..."

Her slim skirt hindering her movement just enough to cause a pleasant swaying of her hips as she walked, the woman glided to the reception desk. Spencer watched as she ran a tapered, unpolished fingernail down a column in an appointment book, then shook her head, her honey-colored pageboy skimming the collar of her ivory linen suit. When she lifted concerned eyes to him, Spencer calmly noted that she was beautiful. Exceptionally.

"Actually, I'm afraid we're booked for the rest of the day," she said with a sigh. "When can we reschedule?"

But then, beauty only went so far.

"Reschedule?" Spencer gave a short, unamused laugh. "Oh, no, no, no. I need to take care of this *today*." He pulled his six-foot-four frame to its straightest and fixed her with what he figured was his most intimidating expression.

The space between her light brown eyebrows puckered, almost imperceptibly. "I'm really very sorry, Mr.—" she checked the name in the book "—Mr. Lockhart. But that's simply not possible."

"My dear, I don't think you understand who you're dealing with." He raised his chin. "Please run and get me the owner or manager, or whoever's in charge, so we can get this straightened out."

He saw the color flare in her pale cheeks; her eyes sparked, for just a moment, before settling unexpectedly into a twinkle of amusement. "I'm afraid I can't do that."

"And why not, may I ask?"

She straightened behind the desk to *her* full height, which, in her high heels, made her only a few inches shorter than he. She extended her hand, her full-blown smile now lighting up her face like the sun. "Brianna Fairchild, owner *and* manager of this fine establishment, Mr. Lockhart. Your appointment was to have been with me. Now, as I was saying…when can we reschedule?" She bent over the book again, a pen poised in her hand.

He refused to let her calculated graciousness throw him off guard.

"Miss…Fairchild, perhaps I haven't made myself clear. I have a very tight schedule, which I just can't change on a whim. I'm a businessman, not some bonbon-nibbling social butterfly."

The smile froze, then faded, as she very slowly leaned forward, bracing her hands on top of the desk. The instant he noticed the glint in her peridot eyes, he realized his mistake.

Never, ever, back the adversary into a corner.

"Mr. Lockhart, please understand something." Her voice was low and steady, but her pique was unmistakable. "As much as I may appreciate your situation, I, too, have a business to run. But I am neither a twin nor a magician. I have appointments for the rest of the day, as I said. And the Franklins *did* arrive on time. Mrs. Franklin is active in at least a half dozen charities, and the bride is a corporate attorney. I assure you that neither of them has much time to sit around munching chocolates. Besides that, trust me when I say that getting twelve bridesmaids together—all of whom have careers of their own—is no mean feat. I'm sure you can understand that it would not be very professional of me to push back clients who *did* arrive on time in order to accommodate *you. Now...*" She tapped the back of the pen into her palm as she straightened, lifting one eyebrow. "When can we reschedule? Or perhaps you would prefer to just let someone else handle your wedding."

"My...?" *If this had been my wedding,* he thought *your impudence would have just cost you a client.*

He expelled a harsh breath. "Well, Miss Fairchild, I guess you have me over a barrel. As my sister has her heart set on your handling all this..." He waved his hand in the air to indicate the whole room and everything it stood for, nauseating as he might find it.

"Your sister?" She cocked her head. "You mean, it's not *your* wedding?"

"Good Lord, no! Not in a million years."

"Oh." He saw her mouth twitch at the corners. From underneath a pair of arched, light brown eyebrows, the cool moss green eyes fixed his in a staring contest. "Well, then, Mr. Lockhart..."

"Well, then, what?"

She spoke as if he was just learning the language. "When can we set up another appointment?"

He paused.

"May I please use your phone? I left mine in my car."

"Of course." She pushed it toward him, expressionless.

Refusing to react to her scrutiny, he punched in the number to his office. "Yes, Mrs. Morgan—am I still free on Friday afternoon? I am?… Good. Would you please block out everything after…oh, just a moment…" He glanced at Miss Fairchild. "Two?"

She checked the appointment book and gave a quick shake of her head. "Two-thirty?"

"Make that two-thirty… Yes…thank you… Yes, I'll be back soon."

She was writing his name in the book when he hung up. "And when is the wedding, Mr. Lockhart?"

He shrugged. "Oh, I don't know. Sometime in May."

With a laugh, she said, "I'm afraid you'll need to be more specific than that."

"Why, for God's sake? It's only February."

"Mmm-hmm." She crossed her slender arms over her rib cage. "And May and June are still the months of choice for Atlanta brides. I'm sure I'll be pretty much booked by the end of the week." She paused, her countenance unreadable. "My services are very much in demand."

"So I've heard." The light from a small brass chandelier directly overhead illuminated her shining hair; he caught himself admiring the way each strand reflected its own particular shade of gold. Quickly averting his gaze, he picked up his briefcase. "I'll call and tell you the date tonight."

"That's fine. If you call after six, you'll get the service. Just leave the information with them. If you don't hear from me, you can assume everything's fine. Oh, one more thing…"

She crossed to a nearby filing cabinet and pulled out a folder, removing some printed pages that she handed to him with an impersonal smile. "Here's a description of all our services with the corresponding fees, as well as payment and deposit requirements. As you can see, we can handle as much or as little of your sister's wedding as she wishes, and our prices are tiered accordingly. Look this over when you get a chance, and we'll discuss this on Friday when we meet.''

"Yes…Friday, two-thirty." He allowed a distracted glimpse at the papers, then clicked open his briefcase, slipped them in, and snapped it shut. He started toward the door, then stepped back to the desk. "Did you say the Franklin wedding?"

"I'm handling Allison Franklin's wedding, yes. Do you know them?"

"Yes. Yes, I do. Family friends."

His father, who had passed away five years ago, and Sam Franklin had been friends since high school. The Franklins were known for their expensive but impeccable taste, as well as their difficulty to please. His mother had at least two "refugees" from Delia Franklin's household staff now happily working for her.

Spencer surveyed Brianna Fairchild with renewed interest. She was as calm and fresh as an early summer morning, even though she was, at that very moment in fact, working with one of Atlanta's most persnickety families. He was tempted to be impressed.

He allowed a brief nod in Miss Fairchild's direction, then forced his thoughts to switch over to that afternoon's distributors' meeting before he was even completely out the door.

Brianna nearly tripped over Delia Franklin when she turned around.

"Mrs. Franklin! I didn't see you there!" She put her hand on the tiny woman's shoulder. "I'm so sorry to have kept you waiting."

Several delicate gold bracelets jingled on Mrs. Franklin's bony wrist as she waved her hand. "Nonsense. I've been *more* than occupied going through all those invitation sample books. I'm positively overwhelmed with all the choices." Her eyebrows vanishing underneath stiff, bottle-brunette bangs, she asked in an unnecessary whisper, "Was that Spencer Lockhart just leaving?"

"Was it ever." Brianna shook her head as she lead the older woman back to one of the conference rooms. "Talk about being impressed with yourself."

Mrs. Franklin's tinkling laugh floated around Brianna's head. "He has a right to be, I guess." She settled herself on one side of the conference table, readjusting her reading glasses on the bridge of her nose, which she then ignored by peering over them. "You've heard of Lockhart and Stern, I assume?"

"Proctor and Gamble's biggest competitor? Of course..." She made the connection. "You mean, Spencer Lockhart is related to the family?"

"He's not *related* to, honey—he *is* that family."

Brianna frowned. "I thought the company was a huge conglomerate."

Mrs. Franklin nodded. "Oh, it is, it *is*. But what most people don't know is that the Lockharts *buy out* the companies that come to L and S, not *merge*. And the family—which is only Spencer, his mother, and little sister—still hold controlling shares of the stock. It's very much *his* company." Mrs. Franklin licked her finger and flipped the page of the sample book in front of her, then swiveled the book around to Brianna, jabbing at a sample with a slightly chipped coral fingernail.

"This one, I'm sure."

When Brianna reached over to take the book from her, Mrs. Franklin touched her wrist with a diamond-laden left hand. She looked up to meet glittering gray eyes behind the silver-rimmed glasses. "Make nice to him, darlin'. He's *loaded*." Coral lips pulled back into a thin smile. "And single."

Brianna suppressed a sigh at Mrs. Franklin's unsubtle matchmaking attempt, then allowed a wry smile. Somehow she had the distinct feeling that her new client was destined to remain single. At least for the next million years or so. "Now, Mrs. Franklin—you know I make nice to *all* my clients."

Their conversation was interrupted by a combination of irritated muttering and rustling satin as Allison Franklin suddenly appeared in the doorway, her pretty face pinched in distress over a high Alençon neckline. She held up the heavy ivory skirt with both hands and whined, "Miss Fairchild, I have got a meeting with a client in exactly *forty-five* minutes and I *still* can't decide on a dress! Maybe I should just wear my debutante dress and be done with it."

"Over my dead body!" Mrs. Franklin snatched her glasses from her nose, letting them fall to the end of the silver chain around her neck. She pushed herself up from the table and took her much-taller daughter by the elbow, leading her back into the dressing room. "Now, honey, you've let yourself get into a real stew over this. I *told* you that you should have let me stay in the dressing room with you, didn't I? Choosing your wedding dress is just *too* important a decision to make all by yourself."

Traumatized bride number three hundred forty-six. Amused, Brianna followed mother and daughter back into the spacious but somewhat shabby dressing room, now strewn with at least two dozen discarded wedding gowns haphazardly rehung or thrown across the back of the settee and chairs like fallen soldiers. In the middle of the battleground stood a thin, hawk-nosed woman with bleary eyes and spongy, nebulous-color hair, shaking her head.

"I'm sorry, Miss Fairchild," the saleswoman said with a wan smile. "It's just that Miss Allison looks so pretty in all the gowns that she just can't choose."

Brianna smiled at her employee's diplomatic explanation of the situation. Allison Franklin was a hellion, and everyone—including her own mother—knew it. Perhaps the stunning red-head pouting at her reflection in the three-way mirror was dynamite in court or at the negotiations table, but right now she was a basket case and would have no qualms about sending everyone around her to the loony bin, as well.

With a sympathetic touch on the saleswoman's shoulder, Brianna said, "Madge, why don't you go help Betty with the bridesmaids now? We'll take it from here."

Madge flickered a grateful smile, then vanished through the curtained doorway.

Brianna stepped up behind Allison, pulling in the back of the too-large sample gown to give the bride an idea of how it would look in her size. She glanced over Allison's shoulder into the mirror, for a moment startled at how much older she seemed than the bride, who was only a few years her junior.

Shifting her focus back to the bride's face, she said in a soothing tone, "Okay, Allison—let's take this step by step. Do you like the lace?"

Allison hesitated, then nodded.

"How about the high neckline?"

"I—I'm not sure." A deep crease had begun to wedge itself between Allison's brows.

"Have you tried any gowns with a low neckline, then?"

Allison shook her head, her brows dipping to meet the crease. "I don't want to look like some tacky soap-opera bride."

Brianna laughed. "I should hope not!" She let go of the dress and put her hands on Allison's shoulders. "Let's start over. You just relax for a minute—I'll be right back." She gave the young woman's shoulders a little squeeze and left the dressing room.

Most of the sample gowns from the big bridal houses were kept in a large storage room behind the bank of dressing rooms. But there were a dozen or so gowns that Brianna kept on a rack in her office, dresses that she herself had designed, dresses that took a certain type of bride—with a certain type of pocketbook—to pull off. Brianna suspected that Allison Franklin was one of those brides.

She hurriedly poked through the gowns… *Yes. This one.* She pulled the gown down from the rod and removed its cover, then returned to the dressing room. Like a toreador spreading his cape before the bull, Brianna swung the skirt of the gown so that it fanned out over a third of the dressing room floor.

Her hunch had been correct.

"Oh, my *God! Where* did you get this dress?" Allison

clapped her hands to her cheeks, her eyes opening so wide Brianna could see the whites all the way around the violet irises. The bride spun around to her mother, shaking her hands and hopping up and down as if she needed to pay an urgent visit to the ladies' room. "Get me *out* of this thing, Momma! I've got to try on that dress *this instant!*"

As Allison yanked at the dress she was wearing in her frantic effort to get out of it, Brianna draped the new gown over the back of a chair and crossed the room to assist Allison and her mother, just in time to save Mrs. Franklin from being buried alive in twenty yards of ivory satin. Free at last, Allison dashed across the room to the new dress, jerking up her fallen bra strap on the way. Suddenly, however, the bride stood stock-still, then timidly touched one of the balloon sleeves as if afraid it would go *poof!* like a burst soap bubble.

"Oh…" The word was a whisper.

The bride's gaze remained clamped to the gown as Brianna removed the creamy taffeta dress from its hanger and slipped her hands into the bodice, scrunching up the enormous skirt in the crooks of her arms.

"Okay, Allison—arms up!"

She obeyed like an obedient little girl. Brianna dropped the silken gown over her head and shoulders, the skirt tumbling into place with a soft *swoosh* as it billowed out at least a yard in all directions. Brianna expertly moved the full skirt to one side and stepped around to Allison's back, effortlessly negotiating the long row of satin buttons and loops down the back of the gown, in spite of the fact that the bride had begun to tremble. Finally, the back done up, Brianna stepped back and took stock of her handiwork, resting her chin in her hand so no one could see her smug smile.

Not bad.

Allison swept up her long auburn hair into a makeshift chignon on top of her head, then twisted around to see the effect, as thousands of tiny diamantés and seed pearls sewn in delicate patterns on the bodice and antique lace skirt glistened like early morning frost under the overhead lights. The bride's porcelain shoulders and neck were perfectly set off by the wide V-neck of the 1840s style gown, her waist whittled to nearly nothing by the pointed, boned bodice. Letting her hair fall, Allison swished around to face Brianna, her expression rapturous.

"Oh, Miss Fairchild, this is the most beautiful gown in the whole world."

"As well as the most expensive." Mrs. Franklin had stepped up beside her daughter and now held in her palm the price tag dangling from the dress. Allison looked at her mother, then at the tag, then turned back to the mirror with a shrug.

"It's not as if we can't afford it, Momma." Allison's voice was low but her chin was raised. "And Daddy has always said you can have anything you want as long as you're willing to pay for it." She traced a feathery outline of beads with one finger. "And I want this dress."

Two sets of eyes met in the mirror for a long moment, then Mrs. Franklin simply nodded.

"Good! Then we're set," Brianna said. "Let's get you out of the gown, then we'll set up another appointment for your fitting and veil selection."

Brianna helped Allison remove the gown, carefully rehanging it while the bride got dressed, then picked up Allison's folder in order to make notes about the gown. No sooner had the young woman left the dressing room than Brianna felt a light touch on her shoulder. She lifted her eyes to meet Delia Franklin's sparkling gaze.

"Yes, ma'am?"

"Don't you 'yes, ma'am' me, you little fox!" Mrs. Franklin's attempt at sounding stern was pitiful. Besides, the corners of her mouth had tilted into a smile. She wagged a thin index finger at Brianna. "You *knew* she'd love that dress."

Brianna regarded the woman for a moment, then smiled. "Just doing my job, Mrs. Franklin."

The woman squinted at Brianna, then burst out laughing.

"Problem is, you do it too well. Remind me to never get into a poker game with you—you're deadly!"

Brianna grinned as she stood, tucking the folder in her arm. "Then I guess it's lucky for you I'm not a card player."

Mrs. Franklin snorted. She started out of the dressing room, then halted in the doorway, her expression now wistful. "My baby's going to be the prettiest bride in Atlanta, isn't she?" With a victorious cackle, she added, "Folks'll be talking about that dress for *years.*"

"Good night, Miss Fairchild."

Brianna looked up at her employee. "Oh, good night, Madge," she said as she toured the waiting room, straightening up. "I hope Miss Franklin didn't beat you up *too* badly."

The thin woman rolled her eyes. "Oh, I've had worse. But I'm not sure what might have happened if I'd been left alone with her much longer!"

The sudden image of skinny, tame, sixty-plus Madge Roberts strangling Allison Franklin with a tape measure brought a smile to Brianna's lips. "It's a good thing I came in when I did, huh? You have a good evening now—"

"Okay, you stupid folder, I *know* you're in here somewhere."

As the saleswoman shuffled out the door, Brianna laughed at her muttering assistant who was trying to reclaim the reception desk. "Expect it to answer you?"

"You never know," Zoe said with a frown as she flung her long, straight black hair over one shoulder. "Stranger things have happened around this place."

Brianna kicked off her heels and dropped into the overstuffed chair in front of the desk. "Speaking of strange—you sure picked a rotten time to go to lunch today."

The girl knuckled one hand into her hip. "Oh, gee, at two-thirty, for twenty minutes. How thoughtless of me." Her black eyes wandered over to the file cabinet under the window a few feet away. "*There* it is. And what doofus put you over here?'' She pushed up the sleeves of her thigh-length, charcoal gray sweater—which the petite girl wore as a dress—and snatched the folder off the cabinet as if it were an errant child being pulled away from the playground. "And when I get back," she continued without missing a beat, "a tornado had touched down on my desk, you managed to sell dragon-bride a dress that costs as much as a small car, and some oinker tried to pick a fight with you because *he's* late for his appointment. Takes talent, lady." Zoe smacked the pile of folders on her desk into a stack with the palms of her hands, then plopped them into a standing file.

Brianna allowed a fond smile for her assistant. "That's me." Then she sighed, sweeping her hair up off the back of her neck with her hand. "Good Lord—if it's this nuts in February, just think what May and June will be like." With a yawn, she added, "I don't think I remember what it's like to have a life anymore."

Her assistant smirked as her small, perpetually moving hands opened drawers, put things in them, closed them, rearranged the phone, put pencils in the cup by the phone, clicked off the charge-card machine. Her speech was as rapid as her movements, always reminding Brianna of the clattering of an old typewriter. "Yeah, well, I just keep thinking about all the *lovely* tips those nice, society brides' mothers give me for dressing their daughters. Money first, life later."

Brianna slid down further into the chair, nestling her head against the back. "What would I do without you, Miss Chan?"

Zoe seemed to consider this for a minute. "Oh, I don't know. Sell the business and retire to Tahiti?"

"Not a chance. This is far too much fun. Besides, I hate sand. Wait a minute—isn't this the twenty-first?"

"Yeah. So?"

"Exactly one year ago tomorrow, you walked in and asked me for a job, remember?"

Zoe wrinkled her nose. "Puh-lease—don't remind me." A half dozen turquoise rings gleamed in the light given off by the brass lamp on the back of the desk as she wagged her finger at her employer. "I never will forgive you for not telling me that I was the fourth person to have the job in less than two years."

"So sue me. You're still here."

The hand dropped. "Yeah, well..."

The phone rang, making both women jump. Zoe glanced at the clock on her desk, then shrugged and picked up the receiver.

"Just a minute—I'll see if she's still here."

Zoe punched the Hold button, but clasped the receiver against her chest anyway. "Spencer Lockhart?"

"Oh, brother." With a laconic gesture, Brianna reached for the phone. Zoe plunked it into her hand, then leaned back against the front of the desk with her arms folded across her chest, settling in for a little blatant eavesdropping.

"Yes, Mr. Lockhart?"

"I'm glad I caught you, Miss Fairchild." His clear baritone voice was more compelling over the phone. "I've got the date for you."

"Oh, yes..." She mimed to Zoe to give her her personal appointment book. The girl pulled it out of the bottom desk drawer and tossed it across the desk into Brianna's lap. She grimaced, then glared at Zoe's unrepentant grin as she flipped the pages to May. "Now...when is the wedding?"

"May twenty-third. Saturday."

Brianna caught her breath. "I don't believe this. Every slot for three weeks on both sides of the twenty-third is already booked, but that day is open."

"Good," came the unimpressed response on the other end of the line. "Put us down for the whole day."

"Oh...but I usually do two weddings on Saturdays..."

"Yes, yes, I know... I read the little treatise on your fees, and I'm aware that you levy a hefty surcharge for being there for the whole day." He paused. "If it's not a problem for you, I can assure you it's no problem for me."

Brianna mugged at Zoe as she replied in her most courteous voice, "Of course not, Mr. Lockhart. No problem at all."

"Good. Then we can make further arrangements on Friday."

"Yes...that will be fine."

"By the way, Miss Fairchild..." Brianna could almost hear his sardonic smile through the phone. "I was very impressed with the information you gave me. In fact, I'm considering sending a couple of my company attorneys to you for instruction on how to write contracts."

She hesitated a moment, then replied, "Why, thank you, Mr. Lockhart. It's so nice to have someone of your business acumen compliment the efforts of a small-business person like me."

Like *little ol' me,* she wanted to say, thickening her accent to the consistency of banana pudding. If he had been standing in front of her, she would have been tempted to flutter her lashes. *That's just what you think, isn't it, Spencer Lockhart? That I'm just some Southern belle playing at running a business, when I should really be home with twenty kids and a nice hubby to take care of me.*

"Not at all," the low voice replied. She started, then realized his response was to what she had *said,* not what she had just thought. There was a chilly pause, then; "Until Friday, Miss Fairchild."

"Yes, of course. Good night, Mr. Lockhart." She handed the phone back to the twitching Zoe.

"Like, what was all that about?"

"Like, I'm not entirely sure, Miss Nosy."

Zoe stuck out her tongue at Brianna, a gesture she made at least a dozen times a day. Then, shaking her head, she walked over to the closet by the front door. "I can't wait to meet this guy," she said as she yanked her down-filled coat off a hanger and shimmied into it, pulling her hair out from the collar.

"Why?"

Zoe crammed a beat-up felt hat with a floppy brim down over her forehead so far she had to lift her head to see Brianna.

"Because…" She hitched a satchel nearly as large as she was up onto her shoulder. Then she shrugged. "Never mind."

"Zoe…"

But the girl just grinned. "Well, I'm gone. Got two classes tonight.

Hey…" Zoe opened the front door, shuddering at the damp, chilled air that greeted her. "When I graduate in June, I expect a raise, you know. If not a promotion."

Brianna rubbed her hands over her arms as the draught made its way over to the chair. "Sure, whatever. Just close the door before I freeze my buns off."

"You can't do that—there's nothing there to freeze off!" Laughing, Zoe pulled the door shut behind her.

Smartass, Brianna thought with a half smile as she heard her own yawn in the vast silence that followed in the wake of Zoe's departure. The soft, rhythmic ticking of the mantel clock on the other side of the room was suddenly the only other sound in the building, just like it was at the end of every day.

Sometimes the soundlessness in the evenings enveloped her like a hug from an old friend; other times, it became a void, as if all the air, as well as the sound, had been sucked out of the room. Which would it be tonight? With another yawn, she decided she didn't care. She was so tired, she'd probably be in bed by nine anyway.

She hauled herself out of the soft chair and went from door to door checking the locks, before padding in her stockinged feet up the circular staircase to her large apartment on the second floor. The thought crossed her mind as she switched on a couple of lamps in her living room that her mother would be amused that, three college degrees notwithstanding, Brianna basically still lived above the shop.

A contented sigh fell from her lips as her eyes whisked over her living room, all done in dark greens and golds and cinnamons. Not a shred of pink anywhere. God, she hated the decor in the salon. But she'd been so busy since she took over the business three years before that she hadn't had a chance to shut it down and redecorate. Maybe in the fall. She shook her head, remembering the peeling wallpaper she'd noticed today in the largest dressing room. *Definitely* in the fall.

Now it was too quiet. Brianna switched on the television without checking the station, then walked across the thick Persian rug—one of the few things in her apartment she'd taken from her parents' house after her father's death—into her bedroom. The drone from the TV kept her company as she went through her nightly routine. She removed her linen suit and immediately hung it up on a sturdy wooden hanger, then shucked off her panty hose and slip, tossing them into the sink of the adjacent bathroom to rinse out later. Shivering a little, she quickly slipped on a pair of heather blue sweats, which had been neatly folded and waiting on the armchair by her bed where she had left them the night before, then scuffed on a pair of sheepskin slippers on her way back to the kitchen.

As usual, dinner was straightforward, uncomplicated: a single portion of frozen lasagna rejuvenated in the microwave, a small salad hurriedly thrown together. She opened the refrigerator to get out a carton of milk, grinning at the sight of the red-and-white Sara Lee carton on the second shelf. *Mmm*, she thought, wiping some olive oil from her fingers. If she cleaned her plate, like a good girl, there was cheesecake for dessert.

She carried dinner into the living room and set it on the coffee table in front of the television, then settled, Japanese style, on the floor at the table to eat. A local news show. Okay, whatever. She took a bite of lasagna and looked up—right into Spencer Lockhart's cobalt eyes.

She banged her knee into the coffee table when she twisted herself around, tossing aside assorted pillows as she pawed for the remote in the crevices of the sofa. Rubbing her knee, she flipped back and aimed the remote at the TV as if she were about to shoot it, clicking the Volume button.

There he stood, surrounded by a group of Japanese executives. Gulliver among the Lilliputians, she thought. Good God—how tall was this guy? Brianna was nearly five-ten herself. She tried to remember standing in front of him earlier.

She *had* had to look up, she recalled. So that meant he was at least six-three, six-four...

Ah...Lockhart and Stern had just negotiated a huge trade deal with a Japanese importer. Pushing a forkful of salad into her mouth, she smiled. VCRs for toilet paper. Sounded balanced to her.

Her jaws efficiently worked on the salad as she studied the overlarge face on the screen in front of her. Yep...she could just sit here and stare and stare and stare, and he'd never even know it. Not a bad face, actually. She quirked her mouth to one side. Actually, it was a very *nice* face. Perfectly proportioned nose, well-defined cheekbones and strong jaw, the chin clefted just enough to make it interesting. Just the slightest traces of crow's-feet at the corners of those brilliant blue eyes, which glittered like jewels under his silver hair.

Not blond. Silver.

It really was gray, wasn't it? Funny, she hadn't noticed earlier in the day, and yet, next to his eyes, it was his most striking feature. She wondered how old he was. Early forties? Not more than that, surely...

As if in answer, the camera focused on the interviewer who was just commenting that, at thirty-six, Spencer Lockhart had assumed an unusually influential role in the international businessworld.

Thirty-six? But that meant he was only three years older than she...

The interview was over. Brianna idly clicked through the other channels, then punched the Off button.

It was dead quiet.

She shut her eyes against the pounding silence, broken only by the intermittent sound of a car passing, the sound of her own breathing.

This was ridiculous. She needed something to watch, or do, or talk to. Next week, maybe she'd go to the pound, get a cat. Or a dog. No, dogs took too much care. She could handle a cat.

Ignoring the panicked racing of her heart, she got up, turned on the radio to the classical station, then collected her dirty dishes and carried them to the kitchen, thinking about names for cats as the strains of a Shubert symphony began to take the edge off her nerves. If she got a gray kitty—a gray kitty with an *attitude*—maybe she'd name it *Lockhart,* she thought to herself with a little laugh.

She washed up the single plate and bowl and set them in the drainer, just as she did every evening. Except that this evening, the image of a pair of brilliant blue eyes kept popping into her head.

She stood in front of her sink, wiping her hands on a dish towel and staring out into the darkness that enshrouded her backyard as she considered the whys and wherefores of her new client. Sizing up people was probably her strongest attribute. That ability had made her an exceptional psychology student and an astute businessperson. Clearly, the arrogance and self-importance Spencer Lockhart showed to the world were just part of his Mr. Business Person costume. She should know—she kept hers in her closet, right next to the suit she had just taken off. But the eyes were real, and they were kind. So very, very kind.

With a sigh, she neatly tucked the towel into its holder on the front of a cabinet door. Then, to her complete surprise, she burst into tears.

2

Spencer shook hands with the interviewer and left the studio, wiping the makeup off with his handkerchief as he walked down the hall. He hoped it hadn't stained his shirt collar, as he wouldn't have time to change before meeting Charlotte for dinner. The frosty air that slapped him in the face as he swung open the glass door was a godsend after the heat of the camera lights.

He liked cold weather, although he found Atlanta's non-committal winters more of a nuisance than anything else—enough sleet or freezing rain to make driving even more of a challenge than it already was, but hardly ever any snow. There'd been a lot of snow up north recently, he mused as he got into the Towncar. He'd bet the Connecticut house looked like a Currier and Ives' print right now. Maybe he could talk Charlotte into flying up with him for the weekend.

He pulled the car up in front of the ritzy hotel where Charlotte had asked him to make dinner reservations, exchanging a word or two with the valet when he handed him the keys. As he crossed the elegant lobby toward the broad staircase leading to the restaurant, he could feel the stares and nods and whispers which were anathema to him, but were Charlotte's lifeblood. Granted, this was one of the finest restaurants in town, and he had no complaints about either the superb food or gracious service. But once in a while he wouldn't mind having dinner someplace a little less conspicuous.

But then, he thought with a chuckle, catching sight of Charlotte as the maître d' led him to the candlelit table, if he'd wanted anonymity, he'd clearly picked the wrong girlfriend. Keeping such beauty under wraps would be damn near impossible.

Her creamy white, unblemished skin was a perfect foil for her thick sable hair, done up tonight on top of her head with soft tendrils grazing her jaw and partially exposed shoulders. To better showcase her ample cleavage, she wore a low-cut dinner suit the color of holly berries, a startling contrast to the muted greens and golds of the restaurant.

She flashed a smile at him as he approached the table.

"Darlin'! Where *have* you been?"

Spencer leaned over and delicately pecked Charlotte's perfectly made-up cheek, his nostrils flaring at her heavy perfume. He didn't recognize the scent, and decided that he did not particularly like it. But it suited her—dark and sensual, a little aloof. He sat next to her at the small but highly visible corner table. "Sorry. Traffic."

"Well, never mind." She pursed her full lips and made a motion of kissing the tip of her finger, then touched the finger to Spencer's cheek. "I ordered your drink for you. I'm on my second." She tapped the glass of her Manhattan with one long, red fingernail, an exact match to her suit.

Spencer frowned. "Just go easy, my dear."

Charlotte held one hand to her breasts, her marquise-cut dinner ring twinkling in the candlelight. "I promise, no more tonight. How did the interview go?" She picked up her menu.

"Fine." He knew she wasn't really interested. When it came to discussing his business, what passed for conversation between them was often little more than an exercise in politeness. As Charlotte had never worked, would probably never need to work, a day in her enchanted life, the intricacies of commerce did not capture her imagination.

Spencer opened his menu, as well, though his thoughts seemed more determined to center on Charlotte than what he'd like for dinner that evening. Their year-long relationship—the first alliance of any duration that Spencer had allowed in quite some time—had become more of a habit than anything else, he suspected. It was comfortable, undemanding. Charlotte was pretty, intelligent, and usually pleasant company, and he truly enjoyed having her on his arm for the many functions he had to attend. No complaints about her in bed, either, the rare times she'd been amenable. As for Charlotte, she clearly enjoyed the cachet that came from being considered Spencer Lockhart's girlfriend. But *love* had nothing to do with it, which made things blissfully uncomplicated as far as he was concerned. The emotional distance she allowed him to keep from her was more than worth the inconvenience of Charlotte's occasional overindulged behavior.

"You ready to order, darlin'?" Her voice seemed to be coming from under water.

"What? Oh... Yes, I suppose so."

"Good." She allowed a flirtatious smile for the young, handsome waiter, then said in a honeyed purr, "I'll have the broiled sole with capers and lemon sauce, a plain baked potato, and a salad, please. No dressing." Charlotte handed the menu to the waiter, her even white teeth gleaming between shimmering holly-berry red lips.

"And for the gentleman?"

"I'll just have the filet mignon with broiled mushrooms. Rare. And a baked potato with sour cream and chives."

"Salad, sir?"

"Yes. Roquefort dressing, please."

"Very good, sir." The waiter took Spencer's menu, nodded, then seemed to float away.

Charlotte laughed softly and shook her head, her ruby-and-diamond earrings, Spencer's birthday gift to her just last month, casting tiny shards of reflected light across her cheeks. "Honestly, Spencer, you *are* in a rut," she teased. "There are other things to eat besides steak."

"None that I care to try at the moment, thank you."

Charlotte grazed her fingernail down his lapel, peering at him from under her dark lashes. "You know so much red meat isn't good for you. And, after all, you convinced *me* to quit smoking.''

Spencer studied Charlotte's pretty, smiling face and felt a twinge of guilt. Maybe he didn't believe in romantic love, but his girlfriend still deserved to be more than just *convenient*. Even he had to admit that the relationship wouldn't have lasted this long had he not been genuinely fond of the woman.

He took her hand in both of his and pressed his lips to her smooth, white knuckles. ''Yes, I did, my little mother hen.'' With one eyebrow cocked and a mischievous grin on his lips, he whispered, ''How about spending the weekend with me at the Connecticut house?''

She shuddered, then said with a borderline pout, ''It's draughty there. And there's nothing to do.''

Spencer leaned forward, placing his arm on the back of her chair. He lowered his voice, his breath teasing one of the tendrils in front of her ear. ''Oh, I imagine I could think of something to keep us occupied.'' He kissed the tips of her fingers, one by one. ''And more than warm enough.''

''Uh-uh, you naughty boy!'' Charlotte giggled and removed her hand from his, clasping her drink. After a moment of silence, she lowered her thick lashes and said, ''Make it the Fifth Avenue penthouse instead, so I can go shopping in the city, and I'll do whatever you want.'' The red lips hitched into a crooked smile as the lashes fluttered back up. ''I promise.''

Spencer looked steadily at her, his fingers tightening around his glass. Then he sat back, gulping the rest of his drink. ''Forget it.''

With as much of a frown as she would allow, Charlotte leaned toward him and put her hand over his, running the tip of her finger up under his cuff and stroking his wrist. ''I'm sorry, darlin'. I didn't mean…'' On a long sigh, she said, ''It's just…I really don't *like* the country house, Spence. And I haven't been to New York in *so* long.'' She slanted her deep brown eyes back up at him. ''But if it means so much to you…''

God, the woman had eyes like a Beagle.

"No, no, no…" He sighed, feeling himself drown in her manipulation. Again. "If you want to go to New York, we'll go to New York. It's no big deal."

Charlotte's eyes lit up as she put her hands on either side of Spencer's face and kissed him—barely—on the mouth. "Oh, thank you, honey." She sat back in her seat, just in time for them to be served their salads. "And I promise, you won't be disappointed."

Spencer picked up his salad fork, its weight like lead in his hand. Unable to eat, he twirled the fork around in his fingers, watching Charlotte pierce a cherry tomato with her fork and lift it to her lips.

The two shades of red clashed.

A slow smile spread across his face. For some reason, he now felt much better.

He was ten minutes early this time. The pretty little Asian girl had asked him to take a seat, assuring him that Miss Fairchild would be with him shortly. And so here he was, sitting in the same Garden from Hell chair. At least there was no magpie convention today.

The room was too warm. The calendar said the end of February, but the temperature outside was pushing spring, having unexpectedly risen nearly twenty degrees since morning. He got up, removed his topcoat, and sat down again, folding the coat across his lap. He propped his elbow on the arm of the chair and rested the side of his face in his hand, then crossed his arms instead, only to uncross his arms and cross his legs.

Suddenly Miss Fairchild appeared, her hand extended to him, her unaffected smile as bright as her sagebrush green eyes. A silky oversize sweater, nearly the same color as her eyes, fell to her hips over a matching ankle-length skirt, its fullness masking her slim figure. Around her slender neck hung a delicate brass-and-amber necklace that softly jangled whenever she moved.

"I know it's a little early, but we might as well get started.

No sense keeping you waiting, after all," she said in a voice as light as a breeze.

Spencer shifted his topcoat to his left arm as he rose from the chair, then shook her hand. It was warm and soft, her handshake firm. He withdrew his own hand as if he'd been shocked.

If she noticed anything precipitous about his behavior, she didn't let on. "Zoe, would you please take Mr. Lockhart's coat?" Then to him, "And would you like something to drink—tea, coffee?"

He felt the coat being removed from his arm. "Uh...coffee, thank you. Black, please," he said to the retreating young assistant, who allowed a brief glance in his direction, her lips posed in a smile that her black eyes did not echo.

Puzzled, but only slightly, by the girl's reaction, Spencer followed Miss Fairchild down a short hallway. Unlike many tall women whose stature made them self-conscious, and therefore awkward, this woman moved like a sleek cat, her full skirt clinging to her long legs as she walked in front of him. Maybe she'd been a dancer...

He stepped through the door into her office.

"I'll be damned—it's not pink," fell right out of his mouth.

"Did you say something, Mr. Lockhart?"

"Oh...just that..." He had not meant for her to hear him. "The colors are very different in here."

With a glint of amusement in her eyes, Miss Fairchild stepped behind her desk, bidding him to sit in one of the bargello-patterned wing chairs on the other side. "Isn't that relentless pink out in the salon the most atrocious thing you've ever seen?" She threw up her hands as if surrendering, musical laughter bubbling out of her throat. "Trust me, I'm not responsible."

Her laughter was infectious. Spencer smiled as he settled himself in one of the chairs, propping one ankle on his knee. "Well, that's a relief. I guess I do remember my sister saying that she thought you'd taken over the business from someone else?"

She nodded. "I bought the business—which included the building—about three years ago. Before that, the place had gone under the name of *Luella's,* after Luella Martin who ran the shop for some forty years. Her business had been quite successful, but her husband was pushing her to retire so they could move to Virginia to be closer to their kids and grandchildren." She stopped suddenly, her hand to her lips. "I'm sorry. I'm sure you're not at all interested in this…"

"No, no—please continue," Spencer urged. "So this was old Luella Martin's place. I had no idea."

"You knew of it?"

"I'm pretty sure my mother had purchased some evening gowns from her over the years. I seem to remember seeing the boxes occasionally."

"Well, Miss Luella didn't know what she had here. I got a great deal."

Always the businessman, Spencer was immediately intrigued. "Oh?"

The young woman leaned back in her chair, her slim fingers playing with one of the smooth stones in her necklace. "Luella sold dresses, period. Her brides, and their mothers, were forced to go all over town for the flowers, the caterers, the photographers. She already had many of the best families coming to her for their outfits—often the daughters bought their gowns from Luella because their mothers had—but didn't realize the potential gold mine dangling in front of her nose."

"And you did?"

She nodded. "It didn't take me more than five minutes to realize that people would gladly pay a premium to have someone else handle and coordinate all the thousands of details that are part and parcel of throwing a wedding." She shrugged. "Not that I was sure that being a wedding planner was what I had in mind. I had come into enough money at the time to go into business, and actually thought maybe I'd open a boutique, something like that. Then I saw the ad in the paper for this place, and arranged an interview more out of curiosity than anything else. But…I wasn't sure. So I told the couple I'd think about it.''

''And that brought down the price.''

She laughed, presumably at his immediate assessment of the situation. ''Dramatically. No one else had even come to see it, and *Mr.* Luella, it turns out, is not a patient man.'' Casting a brief glance out the window, she continued. ''The house alone is worth more than I paid for the whole shootin' match. And, as I suspected, providing a full wedding planning service proved to be just the ticket.'' She pursed her lips, as if deciding whether to continue, then grinned. ''I had made back my investment within six months.''

He could tell she wasn't padding the truth. With an appreciative nod, he said, ''Sounds as though you did very well indeed.'' He nodded toward the hallway, indicating the rest of the salon. ''I take it the, uh, *charming* decor was Luella's idea of *chic,* then?''

''Mmm-hmm.''

''Why haven't you changed it?''

She brushed a wisp of hair back up into her French twist and said with a small shrug of her shoulders, ''There's simply been no time. Oh, good…'' She smiled at Zoe who had just come in with a tray and cups. ''Here's our coffee.''

Just as she reached for her cup, the phone rang. Zoe reached over the desk and picked it up, handed it to Brianna with a sigh, then left the office.

''Yes, Mrs. Crosby? O-okay—ju—just let me put you on hold for *one* second—yes, Mrs. Crosby, I—I'll be right back.'' She punched the Hold button and cradled the receiver against her chest.

''I'm so sorry—do you mind if I take this?'' Lowering her voice, as if not quite trusting the Hold button, she explained, ''A particularly edgy mother-of-the-bride. Needs frequent doses of TLC, but fortunately never wants to talk long.''

He waved toward the phone. ''Please—go right ahead.''

As he half listened to the pacifying voice across the desk,

his eyes took in the room, which could easily have been cluttered had not each item been so deliberately placed.

The horrid mauve carpeting that seeped into the room had been nearly obliterated by an enormous hand-carved Chinese rug, which disappeared underneath the scrupulously neat mahogany desk in front of him. Off-white shelves took up the entire wall behind her desk, filled with magazines, file holders, large glass containers containing paintbrushes and pencils, an occasional plant or statue, and hundreds of books all soldiered on their ends. A short rack stood near the back of the room with several wedding gowns in plastic covers; next to that, a mannequin modeled what appeared to be a half-finished dress, bits of different laces pinned here and there to it like messages on a bulletin board. The walls, the same ivory as the shelves, were peppered with dozens of framed vintage fashion plates, as well as at least half a dozen corkboards with photos, magazine pages, sketches, and fabric swatches placed with military precision.

He sipped his coffee, thinking of their earlier conversation about the business, the price lists that she had given him. From what he could tell, Brianna Fairchild was orderly to a fault. Just like he was. And hardly the image he'd had in mind of a wedding consultant, he thought with an appreciative smile, discreetly studying her out of the corner of his eye. He'd pictured some embalmed matron with scorching red hair and a chiffon scarf sashed around her neck, waxing rhapsodic in a strident voice about palettes and ice sculptures and hundreds of doves. Somehow he had the feeling that this woman didn't do doves. Not willingly, anyway.

He heard the rattle of the phone being hung up.

"Okay—I'm back." Miss Fairchild lightly smacked the palms of her hands on the edge of her desk and let out a sharp sigh, staring at the phone as if it were a rattlesnake. "I swear, some of these women would try the patience of a saint," she said, more or less to herself.

Amused, Spencer propped his elbow on the arm of the chair

and rested his chin in his hand, a half-smile tugging at his lips. "And I take it you're not?"

She looked up at him, slightly started, as if she'd forgotten she wasn't alone. Then she laughed, pushing up her sleeves. "Not hardly—but please don't tell my customers. I wouldn't want to dispel their illusions. *Now,* Mr. Lockhart, let's get back to you…" She twisted around and pulled a crisp, clean manila folder with information blocks already printed on it from the shelf, then picked up a pen lying in front of her on the desk. "My goodness—I don't even know your sister's name yet."

"It's Kelly." He sat back in the chair, tenting his fingers in front of his lips, analyzing her just as he might any new business associate. Except his appraisal of her was hardly businesslike. She had an air of old-fashioned elegance about her, the upswept hairstyle emphasizing her long, slender neck, high cheekbones and surprisingly sturdy jawline that culminated in a precise little chin that could only be called *perky.* Perhaps it was the chin, or maybe it was the dusting of freckles over her nose and cheeks, but there was something of the pixie about her, too, in spite of her height. She reminded him of a blond Audrey Hepburn, in a funny kind of way. But more real. More approachable.

He was suddenly aware of a pair of huge eyes aimed in his direction, green and gray and gold all swirled together. "Her address?"

"Here—you might as well use the family home address." Spencer took a card from his wallet, flipped it over and wrote on the back of it, then handed it to her. As she leaned across the desk to take the card from him, he noticed her scent, a delicate floral. She smelled like spring.

The necklace scraped softly across the surface of the desk as she wrote—left-handed, he noted—the whiskey-colored stones, like her sleekly coiffured hair, glistening in the rays of sun streaming in from the large, lace-curtained window next to the desk. He nodded toward the card.

"I've put the address in Buckhead, as well as Kelly's phone and fax numbers in New York, on the back."

"In New York? Is she in school there?"

"Yes, in fact, she is. Why do you ask?"

With a loud *ke-chonk,* Miss Fairchild stapled the card to the folder. "I graduated from New York University as well as the Fashion Institute of Technology. I just wondered if your sister might be a student at one of my alma maters."

Spencer forgot her original question. "You have two degrees?"

"Three, actually."

He followed her gesture as she pointed to three framed documents on the opposite wall. B.S., psychology, UNC at Greensboro. B.F.A., fashion design, from FIT. M.B.A. from NYU.

"And you do *this?*" he blurted out.

"*This* happens to make excellent use of all my education." Her eyes twinkled straight into his. "Especially the psych degree."

Spencer returned the look, then smiled. "Yes…if the way you handled Nervous Nelly on the phone a while ago was any indication, you must have been at the top of your class."

Her very pretty lips curved up into a slow smile. "I was."

He realized he was being watched, expected to pick up his end of the conversation. He remembered the original question. "Kelly's finishing up her bachelor's at NYU, as it happens."

"Oh? In what?"

"Languages. She wants to be an interpreter."

"Languages?" Miss Fairchild seemed puzzled. "Why NYU?"

Spencer smiled. "Colin O'Brien."

"I don't…"

"Her fiancé. They met two years ago when Kelly went up with me one weekend. He's the son of a business associate up there. And, as it happens, a graduate assistant in anthropology at NYU." Spencer smiled wryly. "She transferred the next semester. And now they're getting married."

"Ah...must be true love."

Spencer paused. "Yes...I'm sure they think it is."

Brianna had not missed the cynicism behind her client's remark. But then, she told herself, Spencer Lockhart's opinions on love were of no concern to her. Unfazed—or so she told herself—she asked, "Has Kelly decided where she wants the wedding and reception to be held? It may be difficult at this late date booking some of the more prestigious places."

"Ah... There's one thing that won't be a problem. She wants the wedding at our family home."

She nodded. This was not an unusual arrangement, considering the size of many of the homes in Buckhead. "About how many guests, then?"

"I don't know...probably in the neighborhood of twelve to fifteen hundred."

"I see." Swallowing down her reaction, she asked, "I take it, then, that the house is large enough to accommodate an event of that size?"

A huge grin slid across her client's face. "I don't think there will be any problem. But then, you can see it for yourself soon enough."

She wished he'd stop scrutinizing her like that, as if he was trying to figure out what made her tick. Still, she couldn't help feeling flattered. The expression in those bright blue eyes was distinctly appreciative. But not at all flirtatious, she realized, surprised at her disappointment. Or relief. She wasn't sure which.

"Yes...the sooner, the better," she finally responded. "Do you live there?"

"Grew up there. I have a town house closer in. Although the house will be mine at some point." He shifted in his seat. "Our mother is the sole inhabitant, at present. Not counting the servants, of course. But she's in Europe until mid March. It...might be better for you to wait to see it when she's back, if that's all right."

"Of course." Brianna noted the dates on the folder, then

asked, "So...do you know if Kelly plans to get her dress in New York?"

His face twitched. "No. I don't."

"How about her invitations? They could certainly go out from there..."

He shook his head, then shrugged. "I'm afraid I haven't the slightest idea *what* her plans are."

Brianna looked up at him. In spite of the silver hair, the crow's-feet, the parenthetical creases around his mouth, he reminded her of a little boy suddenly stuck on a playground full of girls.

"Mr. Lockhart," she said, trying desperately to keep a straight face. "Perhaps you'd better have Kelly give me a call whenever it's convenient for her. I...don't think you're going to be much help."

He bore those blue eyes into hers for a moment, then started to laugh, low and long and hard, shaking his head. Unnerved, Brianna realized the dynamics of their relationship had just been dramatically altered, as if a huge boulder tottering between them had rolled away.

"No, probably not," he said, still chuckling. "But considering that none of this was my idea to begin with..." Then his eyebrows shot up. "Wait a minute!" He leaned forward in the chair and snapped his fingers. "Of course! How about flying to New York with me this weekend and consulting with Kelly yourself?"

Brianna's stomach cramped. "You mean...tomorrow?"

"No, tonight. I'm flying the jet up for the weekend anyway. How about it?"

Her mouth went dry. "I...don't know. I'm not sure what appointments I have...although I don't have to personally attend any weddings this weekend..." Brianna felt a flush creep up her neck. Sudden changes in plans *always* threw her for a loop. "Besides..." She sighed at the perplexed expression on his face. "It's just that, well...you're a very prominent man, and going away for the weekend with you, alone...Well, it just might attract attention. The wrong kind of attention?"

One side of his mouth hitched up, just a little. "I see. Well, if it eases your conscience, Miss Fairchild, Charlotte Westwood will be with us, as well. She and I have been dating for…some time."

The smile froze on her face.

Well, of course he has a girlfriend, you ninny…

"Oh…then…I guess that makes it okay. Let me just check one thing.…"

Why should that make any difference? It's not as if you're attracted to him or anything, is it?

Ignoring her booming heart, she buzzed Zoe, using the phone rather than the intercom. "What's in the works for tomorrow, kiddo?"

She could hear Zoe flipping the page of the big appointment book. "Nothing much. The Briers are coming in, then there's a couple of fairly insignificant appointments. I'm doing the Madison wedding tomorrow morning. What's up?"

"Listen, call the Briers and reschedule for next week sometime—her wedding's not until August. And Madge and Betty can handle the rest."

"What's going *on*, Brianna?"

"I'm going out of town tonight."

"Wh—"

"I'll talk to you *later*," Brianna said firmly. *"Bye."* She looked up and shrugged, ignoring her stomach's acrobatics. "Well…I guess it's a go."

"Great!" He catapulted out of the chair like a jack-in-the-box. "I'll send a car for you about seven, then, if that's okay? Shall I have the driver pick you up here?"

Brianna nodded, then said, "Mr. Lockhart?"

"Yes?"

"It's not as if I don't trust you…but I do need a retainer, as you know…"

The boulder rolled back with a crash. She saw the brightness in his eyes vanish as he whipped a checkbook out from his pocket. Clearly galled, he leaned on the desk and scribbled out a check, ripped it out of the book and tossed it down in front of her.

"There...I trust that's sufficient?"

His abrupt attitude change was a slap in the face. Feeling like a child who was being chided for something she hadn't done, Brianna began to tremble with resentment as she dared to meet his indignant eyes. She picked up the check, glanced at it, and gave a curt nod. After she put the check in a drawer, she gripped the edge of the desk to steady herself. To her shock and annoyance, she felt tears sting her eyes. But, somehow, she kept her voice controlled.

"Maybe my little business doesn't generate billions of dollars in revenues," she said carefully. "And maybe I don't have thousands of workers on my payroll. But what I do is no less real than what you do, in spite of what you obviously feel is its distasteful nature. I have expenses to meet every week, and I have found that the retainer method keeps me solvent so that I do not look like a fool to either my clients or my suppliers. I am only trying to run my business in a fair and professional manner, and I do not appreciate being made to feel that I am requesting something that I do not deserve."

During this, his attention had never wavered from her face. Anger giving her courage, Brianna continued to meet his stare for several seconds, then watched as the ice slowly melted, the set mouth thaw into a sheepish grin.

He sighed. "You're absolutely right, and I apologize." The unexpected softness of his voice was nearly her undoing. He examined the ceiling for a moment, then brought his focus back to her. "It's just that...this whole wedding business is so...so..." Those blue eyes begged for help, and her animosity vanished.

"Out of your league?"

He pinched the bridge of his nose for moment, then let his hand drop. "Yeah," he expelled on a gust of breath that rolled away the boulder for the last time.

Suddenly aware that she was still clutching the desk for dear life, Brianna peeled her fingers away and moved around to him, lightly touching the sleeve of his navy pinstripe jacket before she realized what she was doing.

"That's what I'm here for. Really—you needn't worry about it another minute. After all..." She walked him to the door. "I'm sure you have more important things to do."

He raised one eyebrow, gave a little grunt in reply, then left her office without another word.

Zoe was in her office within ten seconds.

"Tell, tell." She planted her little bottom on the chair where the man had been sitting not five minutes before.

Brianna threw her a good-natured grin as she entered Kelly Lockhart's information into the computer. "I sure can't accuse you of not taking an interest in the business, can I? Or should I say, *my* business?"

Zoe leaned forward and propped her elbows on the front of Brianna's desk, her long hair swishing around her arms as she nestled her chin in the palms of her hands. "You got that right. You going somewhere with tall, gray, and handsome?"

"Don't get excited. His girlfriend's going, too."

"Girlfriend?" Zoe rolled her eyes, muttered a borderline expletive, then said, "Going *where?*"

"New York. Tonight. Back Sunday." She clicked to save the information she'd just entered, then added, "The man realized he had no business even *attempting* to handle any of this for his sister. So, as she's there and I'm here, he decided the most expedient thing to do would be to fly me up there for a consultation." Brianna shrugged. "Sorry, kiddo. That's it."

Zoe slumped in her chair and grimaced, toying with the ring on her right index finger. "Just be careful."

Brianna shot her a look. "What on earth is that supposed to mean?"

With a sigh, Zoe crossed her legs and started swinging her foot. "I just have a funny feeling about him. And you."

"Are you nuts? I just met the man." She leaned forward. "And he has a girlfriend, which I just pointed out." Brianna hesitated, then asked, "Is it the same sort of funny feeling you had about Tom Zimmerman?"

"No way. Those vibes were sca-*ry*."

Brianna nodded. "And these?"

Zoe thought for a moment, then pronounced, "I would say, a serious definite possibility."

Brianna raised one eyebrow. "Is this some holdover from your Chinese heritage, some paranormal ability to see the future?"

"You've been reading too much Amy Tan." Zoe grinned. "I don't talk to ghosts or any of that stuff. This is sheer gut instinct. And the ability to discern when the electron charge goes up in a room when a certain two people share it."

Brianna met her assistant's bright black eyes for a long moment.

"Yeah, right," she finally said, turning back to the computer.

"It's not fair! Why does she have to come with us?" Charlotte folded up a sweater and shoved it into her suitcase.

Spencer put his hands on her arms and nuzzled the back of her neck. "Oh, come on, Char—you're overreacting. It's not as if this has anything to do with our plans."

Charlotte twisted out of his grasp and plunked down on the edge of her bed so hard the suitcase shifted toward her a couple of inches. She clamped her arms across her ribs. "I just thought this was going to be *our* weekend."

Spencer sighed. They spent *plenty* of time alone, if she'd just think about it for a minute. But he knew better than to bring that to her attention. Instead, he sat on the bed next to her, putting his arm around her shoulders.

"It *is*, sweetheart. It's not as if she's going to be sleeping in the same room with us, for God's sake. Besides, she'll be busy with Kelly most of the time. And you're going to spend all day tomorrow shopping. You said so yourself."

Charlotte mulled this over for a moment, then blew out a puff of air from her lips. "Well...I guess you're right." Her pout relaxed into a small smile as she leaned her head on his shoulder. "I'm sorry."

Spencer kissed the top of her head, giving her shoulders a quick squeeze. "There's a good girl. Besides, I think you'll like Miss Fairchild."

Charlotte sighed and stood again to resume her packing, assiduously collecting various items lying about the large Wedgwood blue and white bedroom as if she were a squirrel readying for the winter. "Now, why would I care two *hoots* about Miss Fairchild?" She took a small velvet case from her top dresser drawer, then began selecting which jewelry to put in it.

Spencer laughed in an attempt to assuage Charlotte's sulkiness. "Oh, honestly, Char—you don't have to *care* about the woman. I just thought you might *like* her, that's all. She's a nice lady." Spencer checked his watch. "Are you nearly ready? We need to leave in about ten minutes."

Her back was to him, but he saw her nod, her shoulders tense.

Some fun weekend *this* was going to be.

3

In spite of frequent flights, Brianna still didn't trust airplanes, although she wasn't sure whether it was fear of crashing or throwing up that most concerned her. Whatever it was, by the time the driver deposited her on the tarmac next to Mr. Lockhart's private jet, her stomach was roiling. After three trips up and down the stairs, all the sample books and other paraphernalia she brought with her was stowed away, and she hesitantly entered the main lounge of the plane.

She found an understated collage of masculine grays and beiges accented with brass and charcoal gray granite trim. Her client, almost unbearably handsome in a black turtleneck and beige tweed sportsjacket, was seated in one of a dozen comfortable-looking, high-backed upholstered seats next to a knockout brunette in a glowing teal slacks outfit. Brianna self-consciously tugged at the hem of her favorite fawn-colored velour tunic, half wishing she'd worn something a little classier than five-year-old blue jeans underneath.

"There you are!" He rose from his seat, his voice warm, his smile even warmer. Her heart involuntarily stumbled. "We were beginning to wonder what had happened to you!"

Brianna gave a tiny shrug, heard a nervous laugh crawl out of her throat as she approached the couple. "Wet road, Friday night—unbeatable combination." They shared a knowing laugh in the heat of his companion's glaring inspection of her.

The introductions that followed gave Brianna the opportunity to do some sizing up of her own.

As Brianna extended her hand to Charlotte, she noticed that the brunette had the sort of buxom figure that would probably require lifelong weight-watching. At the moment, though, everything was completely under control, and Brianna imagined the effect on most men was nothing short of mind-boggling.

Charlotte's weak handshake was accompanied by a forced smile and an unenthusiastic, "It's so nice to meet you, Miss Fairchild."

"I'm pleased to meet you, too, Miss Westwood."

Brianna felt a nag of adolescent inferiority as she noted Charlotte's perfect hair and makeup. She unconsciously raked her hand through her own windblown mop and tried to smile again at the seated woman. Apparently she had already received Charlotte's smile allotment for the evening.

"Dinner will be served soon after we take off," Mr. Lockhart said. "Will you join us?"

"Oh...thank you, but I ate before," Brianna lied. Even if her obstreperous stomach would have let her eat, there was no way she was sitting any closer than necessary to Charlotte. "If it's all right with you, I'd like to use the time to work on some designs for an appointment I have early next week. I'll just sit over there." She pointed to an empty seat as far from the couple as possible.

"Of course, I understand. Though I think Charlotte might be disappointed that she won't have another woman to chat with on the flight after all." He lay his hand on his girlfriend's shoulder.

"Yes...that *is* a shame, Miss Fairchild," Charlotte said, suddenly coming to life. She spoke with an italicized inflection that only another Southerner would believe wasn't a put-on. "Spence has told me *so* much about you and your little business. I was really looking forward to hearing *all* about it. But I *do* understand."

Brianna smiled, even more grateful she had chosen to sit where she had. "Thank you. Perhaps we'll get to visit in New York."

"Perhaps we will."

Brianna took her seat, latching her lap belt for the imminent takeoff, her thoughts drifting aimlessly as she tried not to think about what the plane was about to do.

Does she really think that condescending attitude is intimidating? she thought, then sighed. Good Lord, men were dense creatures. Mr. Lockhart had probably told Charlotte all about her, completely clueless as to how women react to unwanted information of that nature. She sucked in her breath and shut her eyes, visualizing her organs being rearranged as the plane left the runway. Well, whatever mess Spencer Lockhart had created with his girlfriend was certainly none of her business.

The aircraft leveled out; as her stomach clawed its way back to its normal position, Brianna reached into her oversize tote bag and pulled out a sketchbook. Quickly becoming lost in her drawing, she did not realize that her work was being watched from over her shoulder.

"That's nice."

She almost didn't hear him over the hum of the engines. Her eyes darted up, then around to where Charlotte was sitting. Herself was flipping through the pages of a magazine, tapping one long fingernail in time to the music apparently coming through the earphones on her head. Satisfied she wasn't being given the evil eye, Brianna allowed a smile for Spencer, then dusted eraser crumbs off the sketch.

"Thank you, I guess. It's not finished."

"It's not?" He knelt beside her, smelling of expensive aftershave with a hint of cedar-lined closets, the pleasant odor heightened, she guessed, because of the closeness in the small plane.

"Nope. The bride wants *lots* of lace."

He wrinkled his nose, a funny expression on such a dignified face. "Why? It's so nice, just the way it is. Simple. Uncomplicated."

"I agree, Mr. Lockhart...."

"Please...Spencer."

"Spencer." She paused, liking how the name sounded on

her tongue, then continued, "But it's my job to give the bride what she wants. And this one wants lace."

She frowned at a seam line she'd drawn, erased it and redrew it, flinching when Spencer tapped her hand to get her attention again.

"Look, I—I want to apologize again for my...rudeness to you earlier. I forget sometimes that not everyone I meet is a potential foe to be subdued and conquered." He looked down at the floor for a moment, then said, "We got off on the wrong foot, I guess. You have an excellent reputation, which is why Kelly wanted me to hire you to begin with. And I've seen proof, already, not only of your excellent business sense, but of your talent." He extended a hand and a smile. "Friends?"

It wasn't difficult to return the smile. "Friends," she agreed, slipping her hand into his without a second thought. Just a business shake, no different from the thousands of others she'd given and received in the past three years.

Then why did her heart lurch into her throat the moment they touched? Why, when they had each reclaimed their own hands, did her gaze linger on his face when he rose?

"I can't tell you how pleased I am that you'll be handling this for our family," he said.

"Me, too."

Brilliant.

"Darlin'?" came a high-pitched wheedle from the back of the plane.

Expressionless, Spencer mouthed the words, "Duty calls," then abruptly returned to his seat.

With a frown, Brianna returned to her work, mulling over the apology. She'd bet her last dollar that he didn't dispense those very frequently. Then her thoughts drifted to his girlfriend. What, she wondered, was a man like Spencer Lockhart doing with the likes of Charlotte Westwood?

And as for her reaction to that handshake—well, she thought, beginning to sketch in where the lace would go on the dress, there was just no explaining *some* things, now was there?

* * *

Brianna stood on the terrace of Spencer's Fifth Avenue penthouse overlooking Central Park briskly rubbing her arms in a futile attempt to ward off the raw February wind that whipped around her, obliterating the remains of the muffled traffic noise twenty stories below. Her gaze followed a ribbon of light threading its way through the park across Sixty-sixth Street as an army of taxis shuttled theatergoers and late-night diners home. Looking out across the park, dotted with street lamps easily visible through bare trees, she could see the steady lights of the Upper West Side, and beyond that, already diffused by a haze of pollution, the flickering ones of New Jersey. Even at night, the view was mesmerizing.

"Hey, there...I'm not partial to the idea of transporting an ice cube back to Atlanta on Sunday." Spencer's low voice rumbled toward her on an icy breeze a half second before he joined her at the railing, his hands knotted into the pockets of his jacket.

Brianna tossed her head. "I'm not cold," she lied. "Besides...I just couldn't wait to see this."

Spencer leaned his elbows on the railing and sighed. "I know what you mean. I've been all over the world, but, corny as it sounds, there's no place that can hold a candle to New York." He faced her, but she couldn't see his expression in the filtered light from the closed French doors behind them. Then he laughed.

"Not cold, my foot. You're shivering so hard you're out of focus. Here..." He took off his jacket and started to put it around her shoulders, but she stopped him with a jerk of her head back toward the apartment.

"I don't think I'd do that if I were you."

He hesitated, then took back the jacket with a short nod. "If you say so. But it's no big deal." He threw it on a nearby chair, as if refusing to be any warmer than she was, then leaned his back against the railing.

Brianna crossed her arms more tightly. "Where is Charlotte, anyway?"

"Gone to bed." He paused. "Alone."

Brianna blushed, even though her client's sleeping arrangements were none of her business. In spite of the darkness that precluded his being able to see her, she looked back out over the city. A sudden gust of wind ruffled her hair as it pierced her tunic. Now her teeth were chattering. "W-what t-time is K-Kelly coming t-tomorrow?" she asked as she tried to smooth back her hair.

"Would you listen to yourself?" Chuckling, Spencer retrieved the jacket from the chair and put it around her again, this time leaving his hands on her shoulders so she couldn't refuse.

It was as if she'd been split in two by a sudden bolt of lightning. Part of her was nearly overwhelmed with the sudden desire to lean back against his broad chest and feel enfolded in his arms, while another part, recently stung, reacted to his innocent touch with panic racing through her veins. Relief and regret wrestled in her head when he dropped his hands.

"Stubborn female," she heard him tease. "We *could* go inside, you know."

"Oh…just one more minute?" she managed to say over the knot in her throat. "The air feels so nice after being in the plane." She snuggled into the wool jacket, fully aware that she was using it as a substitute for the man. A safe substitute. It smelled like him, clean and strong and indefinably masculine.

He acquiesced with a nod, then said, "Kelly'll be here around ten or so, so you can sleep in if you like."

"Sleep in?" Brianna laughed, allowing herself a peek at his face. "Not likely. I've got far too much work to do. By the way—my room is lovely."

"Glad you like it. Even if it isn't pink, huh?" Her heart jumped when he winked at her. Then he stifled a large yawn with his palm. "Listen, you can stay out here and freeze to death, but I think I'm going to turn in, if it's all right with you."

"Of course, please…" She shooed him away with her hand,

then immediately tucked it back against her ribs, nestling under the jacket. "Go on."

He walked over to the doors, but didn't go through. "Now don't…"

She grinned. "I'll come in soon. I promise."

He hesitated.

"Really."

"Okay…" Finally he went inside, leaving the door cracked open so it wouldn't lock.

Brianna sat on one of the patio chairs, pulling his jacket up around her ears. She had been right, she thought with a smug little grin as she once again pushed back a lock of hair that the wind had plastered to her face. He was just as kind as she'd thought he would be when she saw the TV interview that night, saw those wonderful eyes. For a few minutes, she could forget the fear. Heavens—she couldn't remember the last time that anyone had been the least bit concerned about her. Wouldn't it be nice…

Hello? Miss Fantasy-brain? He has a girlfriend, remember?

Her sigh was loud enough to be heard over the wind.

It might have been Brianna's intention to be up no later than seven, but her body had other ideas. When she finally managed to force one eye open, the clock by her much-too-comfortable bed said 9:05. She threw back the covers and shot up out of the bed, only to have to sit back down on the side because she felt dizzy. After her head cleared a moment later, she dashed through her shower and hair and makeup, then stood immobile in her robe in the center of the room, completely unable to decide what to wear.

She dumped the contents of her soft-sided suitcase out on the unmade bed and riffled through her clothes as if they were items on a markdown table, then started to giggle.

"For crying out loud," she muttered to herself. "This isn't an audience with the Queen. Just get dressed and get your butt out there."

She threw on an oversize plum-colored cotton turtleneck

sweater, jeans, and running shoes. She and Kelly would be doing a lot of walking today; the last thing Brianna needed was a pair of sore feet. And she'd long since learned that nobody dressed up in New York unless they absolutely *had* to. Still, she checked her sleeked-back hair in the mirror, splashed on a dollop of perfume, then clipped on a pair of plain gold disk earrings before leaving her room.

The hallway outside reeked of a much heavier perfume than hers, the only evidence that Charlotte had been in the apartment. Somehow, Brianna knew that the brunette was long gone. The overpowering scent, combined with Brianna's empty stomach, made her slightly queasy as she found her way to the kitchen.

Casually attired in a natural wool fisherman's sweater that called even more attention to his broad shoulders, Spencer sat at a small round glass-and-iron table in a bay window at one end of the huge sunny room, cup of coffee in one hand, the *New York Times* in the other. His eyes, twinkling sapphires in the white winter sunshine, lit with amusement when he saw her. Her insides fluttered, though from hunger or the expression in his eyes she couldn't say.

"So...weren't going to sleep in, huh?"

Brianna shrugged, managed a smile. "I lied," she said, sizing up what seemed to be an extraordinary amount of food being prepared on and around the stove. Her stomach growled.

His laugh was relaxed, natural. "Breakfast isn't quite ready yet, though obviously you are. Coffee?"

She nodded. The wrought-iron chair scraped across the tiled floor as she pulled it out and sat opposite him. It would have been impossible not to return the broad smile of the stocky, gray-haired woman who poured the steaming brew into a pretty china cup in front of her.

"Miss Fairchild, this is Colleen O'Hara, without whom this apartment would resemble a frathouse after a Saturday night beer bust."

Brianna had seen most of the apartment by this time. Some frathouse.

"Good mornin', miss," Colleen said in an unapologetic Irish brogue. "Pay no attention to him. He does like to prattle on." Laughing, she returned to the stove, Brianna's eyes following her like a dog's.

"Is Charlotte gone already?" She took a sip of the coffee. It was bitter. She set the cup down.

Spencer folded up his newspaper and put it on the window seat beside him. "Oh, yes. In fact, she should be browbeating her first salesclerk of the day right about now."

Brianna watched as Colleen started carrying plates of food past her into the dining room, her stomach now protesting so loudly she could hardly concentrate on the conversation.

"Beats me why she thinks she's going to get anything in New York she can't get in Atlanta."

"What?" Brianna turned to Spencer. The sun cast a halo around his light hair this morning, at the same time illuminating the tiny lines around his eyes and mouth.

"I'm sorry," she laughed. "I'm just so hungry this morning, my brain is not functioning properly. When did you say Kelly was coming?"

"Any minute."

"Good." She paused. "Will you be joining us for breakfast?"

He shook his head, then finished his cup of coffee. "Unlike *some* people in this apartment, I got up very early. I had breakfast hours ago."

"Oh…"

"Besides, do you really think there's any way I'd want to be in the same room with a bride-to-be and—" he pretended to shudder "—a *wedding consultant?*"

Brianna returned his teasing smile. "No, I guess not." She tried another sip of the coffee. It just wasn't working this morning. Maybe he took it stronger than she was used to. "I suppose this means that you won't come with us when we shop for a dress, either."

"Bingo." He smiled. "We could meet for a late lunch, though. Then you could meet the groom, too."

"And Charlotte?"

Spencer snorted. "Won't surface until the last store closes, believe me." He hesitated. "By the way, she and I have tickets to a show this evening, which I got before I asked you to come with us. I know it seems very rude of me to go off and leave you…"

"Oh, please, forget it!" Brianna shook her head. "As it happens, I was wondering if I'd have a chance to visit a college friend who lives up by Columbia. This will work out perfectly."

"You're sure?"

"Absolutely."

He smiled, relieved. "Good."

Suddenly the doorbell rang, and Brianna heard a clear, sparkling female voice with a flagrant Southern accent exchanging greetings with Colleen, followed by strong footsteps resounding on the parquet floor as the voices neared the kitchen.

"Spence!" A lanky young woman with waist-length, cornsilk-colored hair burst through the swinging door into the kitchen and into Spencer's arms.

"Hey, button!" Brother and sister hugged each other for several seconds, then he turned her around, his arm protectively encircling her slim waist. Matching sets of cobalt eyes now regarded Brianna. "See what I brought for you?" Spencer said to his sister, giving her a little squeeze. "Your very own wedding planner."

As she and Kelly shook hands, Brianna took the opportunity to size up her pretty new client. Like Brianna, Kelly had a boyish figure—no breasts, no hips, no fanny—her thinness now partially concealed by a blousy cambric cowboy shirt replete with fringes and beads, her long blue-jeans-clad legs disappearing into handmade red leather cowboy boots. But this was no tomboy, in spite of her figure and manner of dress. Her delicate features—a more finely proportioned version of her brother's classic lines—nearly translucent skin, and shimmering white-blond hair gave Kelly Lockhart an ethereal beauty that was utterly feminine. She would be an enchanting bride.

Kelly pulled away from her brother's embrace and took Brianna's arm. "Why, Miss Fairchild, you're *much* younger than I thought you would be!" She laughed and tilted her head at her brother, her hand on her hip. "And you tried to make me believe that this would be such a terrible ordeal for you. You would've thought she was an *ogre* or something!" She leaned over and gave him a light slap on his arm. Ignoring the blushes that overtook both Brianna and her brother, Kelly raised her face in the air like a hunting dog and sniffed. "Mmm—French toast?"

Spencer pointed to the dining room.

"Then *why* are we standing in here, for goodness' sake?" Kelly tugged at Brianna's arm, then said to her brother, "You eating with us?"

"You know what they say—three's a crowd."

"Then, *au revoir.*" She wiggled her fingers in a backward wave as she herded Brianna through the kitchen door.

The two women had their plates full before the swinging door between the two rooms had come to a halt. Brianna stole a peek at Kelly's plate and burst out laughing.

"What?" Kelly gave her a good-natured smile as she licked a drop of syrup from a slender finger. Brianna noticed that, in spite of her fairness, her only makeup was a touch of pink lip gloss and a swipe of blush. Even her pale brows and lashes had been left natural.

"It's just that…I'm *so* hungry, I thought I'd look like a prize-winning hog." Brianna nodded toward Kelly's burgeoning plate with a grin. "Seems I'm not alone."

"Oh, God, no." Kelly stuffed half a piece of bacon into her mouth, crunching as she continued speaking. "It's that time of month when I could eat half of New York."

She sat down at one end of the dining table with Brianna to her right. Nearly ten minutes passed before either said anything more substantial than, "Please pass the sugar," as they concentrated on wolfing down their enormous breakfasts. Finally, Brianna sat back with a giggle.

"I think maybe I feel somewhat human again." She poured another glass of orange juice from the pitcher on the table in front of her. "How about you?"

Kelly nodded as Spencer stuck his head into the room.

"I'm going to be in the study if you need me, catching up on some work. Where do you ladies want to meet for lunch?"

Kelly groaned in the direction of her empty plate. "I couldn't possibly think about any more food right now. Besides, I don't know what Miss Fairchild's plans are for me."

Brianna laughed. "No matter what we have to do, trust me—lunch will definitely be on the itinerary. How about…we meet you in front of Bergdorf's at one-thirty? If that's okay with you?" she asked Kelly.

"Sure," Kelly nodded. "If you think we can accomplish enough before then…."

"Trust me," Brianna said again.

"Okay, ladies…see you then." Then Spencer wagged his finger at Kelly. "And don't you dare be late."

With wide eyes, Kelly splayed her hand across her chest. "Trust me."

Kelly waited several seconds after her brother's departure, craning her head toward the door like a robin listening for worms underground. Then she asked, her nose wrinkled in distaste, "What do you think of Charlotte?"

Brianna nearly choked on her orange juice. "Excuse me?"

"I just keep hoping the aliens'll come back for her *real* soon. Don't you?"

Brianna tried hard not to laugh, covering her mouth with her napkin. Finally she murmured, "I really don't think it's my place to say…"

"Nonsense," the blonde retorted, then sighed. "Oh, all right, I shouldn't put you on the spot. It's just…I'd just love to have someone second my opinion that that overdressed floozy is just so *wrong* for Spence…and I can tell he doesn't love her." She grunted. "Not that *that's* any surprise."

Brianna would have given her eyeteeth to press Kelly further on the subject, but she didn't dare. It was, after all, absolutely none of her business.

"More juice?" She held up the pitcher.

With a nod, Kelly held out her empty glass, then blew out a rattly breath as Brianna filled it. Brianna looked up at her client as she set the pitcher down. It had not been a sigh of contentment.

"Does your brother's relationship with Miss Westwood really bother you that much, Miss Lockhart?"

"Yes, it does, though that's not what's eating at me just at the moment." She tilted her head, a little smile curving her thin lips. "And please...call me Kelly. *Nobody* calls me by my last name."

"All right...Kelly..."

"And do you mind if I call you Brianna? It's such a pretty name."

Brianna smiled. "No...not at all." Then she frowned. "So..."

Kelly pushed her plate away from her and stuck her elbow up on the table, resting her chin in her hand. "Oh, I don't know. This whole wedding business..." She shrugged. "It's just not...*me.*"

Brianna felt her eyebrows shoot up. "But...I thought this was *your* idea. That it was you who insisted on hiring me."

"Oh, hiring you *was* my idea." She sighed again, pushing a hank of shimmering hair behind one ear. "In fact, I told Spence and my mother that unless they could secure your services, I wouldn't have anything to do with it."

With a small laugh, Brianna said, "Gee...I'm flattered. I guess. But I don't understand..."

Kelly put her arms up over her head and stretched so hard that Brianna heard the girl's vertebrae crack, then let her hands flop down on the edge of the table. Her fingers fiddled with small creases in the tablecloth as she talked. "It all seems so silly. I mean, Colin and I have been living together for a year. A huge wedding seems so...so *hypocritical,* somehow." She wrinkled her nose again, just like Spencer had done on the plane the night before. "Doesn't it?"

"Is it genetic?"

"Huh?"

"This thing your family has against weddings. Your brother acts as if they're one stepped removed from the plague."

With a flip of her hand, Kelly said, "He's a whole other story...."

Brianna couldn't stand it anymore. "I'm sorry, Kelly, and I know I'm butting in—but twice in the past five minutes you've alluded to your brother's past. I know it's just plain nosiness on my part..."

"He was jilted."

"Pardon?"

A delicate hand clamped onto Brianna's wrist. "Listen— *please* don't tell him I told you. He'd skin me alive if he knew I'd opened my big mouth."

"Of course I won't say anything—"

Kelly forged ahead before the assurance had passed Brianna's lips. "He was stood up at the altar by some lady named Barbara." She sighed. "I was only twelve, but I didn't like *her* either. I kept wishing and wishing that they'd break up, so, when she didn't show, I thought my prayers had been answered. I was happy as a clam until I realized how horribly unhappy Spence was. It took three years of therapy before I finally got it through my thick head that *I* hadn't caused Spencer's heart to break."

Brianna frowned. "So...that's what he's got against weddings," she said, more or less to herself.

"Me, too. I guess we feel like they're bad luck, you know?"

"Then..." Brianna steered the subject back on track, ignoring the pang of sympathy she felt for the man making phone calls in a nearby room. "Who *does* want the big wedding?"

"Our parents, of course." Kelly twisted her mouth to one side. "Colin's from an *enormous* Irish family, and my mother…well, let's just say that if I eloped, I'd be guilty of murder."

"Ah…" Brianna felt a sense of relief. "So you don't have any reservations about marrying Colin."

"Oh, no!" Kelly's eyes widened. "In fact, we'd get married tomorrow if we could do it without upsetting our families."

Brianna hesitated, then leaned forward and put her hand on Kelly's shoulder. "Listen to the older, wiser woman… I figured out a long time ago that weddings, like funerals, are not for the guests of honor. They're for everyone else. The way I see it, my job is twofold. First, I throw a party that'll knock everyone's socks off. Second, I make it as painless as possible for the bride and groom. All you have to do is show up, look pretty, say 'I do,' and leave. Think you can handle that?"

Kelly studied Brianna for a long moment, then nodded. "Yeah. I can do that." She pushed herself out of her chair, leaned over and gave Brianna a hug, then sat down again and grinned. "You're really going to make it okay, aren't you?"

"You betcha, young lady." Brianna pulled over an invitation sample book. "Now—you've got forty-five minutes to choose an invitation. Then we go dress shopping. Get cracking, missy." She pushed the book in front of Kelly and shot her a stern look.

Kelly giggled and opened the book, its cover thudding onto the table.

The two ladies left Saks at one-fourteen, according to Brianna's watch, which gave them exactly sixteen minutes to navigate the Saturday afternoon Fifth Avenue crowd and reach Bergdorf's, eight blocks away, by one-thirty, where they were supposed to meet Spencer and Colin. Tricky, but not impossible.

Giggling so hard they were out of breath, they zigzagged through bundled shoppers, hot dog and chestnut and souvlaki carts perfuming the frosty air with mouth-watering smells, shivering sidewalk peddlers hawking bogus designer handbags in hoarse voices, tourists chattering in a dozen languages standing smack in the middle of the sidewalk with their Nikon cameras pointing skyward.

"There they are!" Kelly shouted to Brianna.

Brianna strained to see over a hundred bobbing heads, skillfully dodging traffic as they skittered across a side street against the light. "Where?"

"Over there! Ohmigosh—I'm so sorry!" Kelly apologized to a glowering woman whom she had just smacked with her full shopping bag. "You can't miss Colin. Red hair!"

Brianna looked again, and indeed, the redhead could have guided ships to safe harbor. When they got close enough to be seen by the two men, Kelly suddenly grabbed Brianna by the wrist, nearly throwing her off balance.

"Slow down," she said, and Brianna understood. With two minutes to spare, they casually approached Spencer and Colin with wide smiles, their breath coming in short white puffs, their hearts racing. The women dared not look at each other for fear they'd burst out laughing.

"Well, well…they *did* make it," Colin teased as he bussed his fiancée's lips, not removing his hands from the pockets of his leather bomber jacket. The rims of his ears were nearly as bright a color as his hair.

"Of *course,* we made it. We're not flakes, you know."

"Of course not," Spencer said, surveying the array of shopping bags in the two ladies' hands. "And is there a bridal gown in any of those bags?"

"No," Kelly replied with a smirk. "They were all from hunger."

"And were they?" Spencer directed toward Brianna.

"Pretty much," she admitted. "But at least I know what Kelly *doesn't* want, so now I can design something for her."

"Neat, huh?" Kelly said, then put her hand on her stomach. "Now for the important stuff. Where should we go for lunch?"

"Anywhere that's nearby. I'm frozen solid." Spencer blew into his hands to warm them, shifting from one foot to another.

Brianna could feel the chill beginning to penetrate her long wool coat as she began to cool off from her dash up the street. She'd forgotten how godawful cold this corner could be this time of year, the feeble white sun eking its way through the buildings as good as useless.

"Well," she said, her teeth chattering. "Anyone g-game for a little Chinese place I used to go to when I was in s-school here? They had the best beef and broccoli in g-garlic sauce in New York." Brianna tried to grin, but her lips were so cold she thought they'd crack. "Guaranteed to take the ch-chill off."

"Sounds great to me. Is it close?" Spencer asked, pulling the collar of his sheepskin jacket up around his neck.

"Seventy-third and Broadway. Short cab ride."

"Fine." He stepped out toward Fifth Avenue, his hand raised in an attempt to flag down one of the hundreds of yellow cabs zooming past them. On their way *down*town. The restaurant was *up*town.

Kelly cupped her hands around her mouth and called out to him. "Oh, Spencer..."

"What?" He whipped his head around to his sister.

Laughing, Colin had one lady on each arm. "I find it's usually more expedient to catch a taxi headed in the *right* direction, brother-to-be." He nodded toward Central Park South, a block away. "C'mon, let's go up to the park and get one going crosstown."

Grumbling, Spencer stuffed his hands further into his pockets and walked away from the curb, startling Brianna by putting his hand through her arm and pulling her away from Colin. As they started toward the park, a sixth sense made her turn partway around. She could have sworn she saw Charlotte standing in front of Bergdorf's with a dozen shopping bags hanging off her arms, watching them with a scowl that made her seem at least ten years older.

4

Charlotte emerged from the bathroom, still in her robe. Spencer had been sitting in an armchair, reading, waiting for her to get ready. He now glanced at his watch and frowned. "Why aren't you dressed?"

With a grimace, Charlotte lowered herself onto the edge of the bed, the deep purple silk jacquard robe falling open to reveal a matching nightgown underneath. "I'm sorry, Spence…"

"What's wrong?" He put down his magazine, thinking with a start how young she looked without her makeup. Which she was. Twenty-five to his thirty-six. Usually he never even thought about it. But tonight…

Her mouth tweaked into a small smile. "I've got a really terrible headache. I took something for it an hour ago, but it just doesn't seem to want to go away." She lifted doleful brown eyes to him. "I'm sorry," she said again, and he got the picture. *Not tonight, dear…I have a headache…*

"Oh…" A little surprised that he actually felt relieved rather than disappointed, he got up and sat beside her on the bed, putting his arm around her shoulders. "Now, don't you think another thing about it. These things happen." He paused. "I take it you don't feel like going to the theater, then?"

She winced when she tried to shake her head, then leaned against his shoulder. "The last thing I feel like doing right now is listening to a hundred people singing at the tops of their lungs."

"Poor baby. You want to get in bed?" At her nod, he stood and started to pull back the covers. "Come on—let's get you tucked in. I'll have Colleen bring you a light dinner and some tea."

He helped her off with her robe and into the bed, propping several pillows behind her back, then started to leave.

"No—wait."

He turned, wondering.

"I...we need to talk."

His skin prickled. Charlotte *never* wanted to talk. "Now? I thought you weren't feeling well..."

"This can't wait," she said, then sighed. "Not anymore."

"Oh?" he asked, unable to fully mask the edge in his voice. "Okay," he said, sitting on the edge of the bed beside her. "What do you want to talk about?"

She lifted those huge hound dog eyes to him. "I think it's time we got married, don't you?"

About six forty-five, Brianna let herself into the penthouse with the key Spencer had lent her, surprised to find him standing in middle of the living room staring at the fireplace with his hands in his pockets, looking like a pigeon that didn't know where to roost. The door's overloud click when it shut it apparently caught his attention.

"Brianna!" His footsteps as he approached her were swallowed up by the thick Turkish carpet that stretched across half the room. "I thought you'd be out the rest of the evening. Here...let me help you with your coat."

She removed her gloves and stiffly unbuttoned her coat. The warmth in the apartment making her icy face sting, she stood for a moment with her hands pressed up to her cheeks. "I could say the same of you. What happened to dinner and the theater?"

A whiff of his aftershave made her slightly giddy as he took her coat from her and draped it over a chair, and she couldn't help but notice the startling contrast of his thick silver hair against the collar of his navy blazer. "Charlotte isn't feeling well, so our plans were canceled.'' There was a sharpness in his voice that made her think he was more agitated than he should be about his girlfriend's being under the weather. ''And you? Why aren't you still with your friends?''

He was standing much too close to her. Fidgeting with a small cameo ring she wore on her right hand, she said, ''I decided a couple of hours was long enough for a visit.'' Her eyes sprinted around the room, seeking an escape of some sort. Then she crossed to a Chippendale side table between two windows swagged in ruby damask to get a better look at a large, intricately carved jade vase.

''Oh?'' He made no attempt to disguise the curiosity in his voice. Ice tinkled against glass as he picked up a drink from the marble mantelpiece. The gesture apparently prodded his hospitality. ''Can I offer you some mineral water?'' As she shook her head, he continued. ''But I thought you'd been such good friends with this woman...''

''I was. Am. And we haven't seen each other since I left New York. But Robin's *husband*...'' She grinned and glanced sideways at him, idly noticing that his nose was not perfectly straight. ''The only two words that come to mind at the moment that adequately describe Giles are *creepy* and *disgusting*. After two hours, I felt a very strong urge to put the man in a jar.''

Spencer chuckled and took a sip of his drink. ''Sounds charming. Seems odd, though, that someone that *you* would consider a good friend could hook up with someone fitting that description.''

Brianna felt a frisson of pleasure at what she decided was his compliment, then shrugged and sank into the corner of one of the matching red damask sofas in the center of the room. ''Makes you wonder, doesn't it?''

The ice rattled again as Spencer set his glass down on a small table, then leaned his elbow on the mantel. ''So now you have your whole evening free. What are you going to do?''

She shook her head, drawing down her brows. ''Oh, I don't

know. I hadn't really thought about it. I suppose I'll just read—I saw several books in your library that called to me.''

Spencer stood straight and rubbed his chin with his hand. "You know...I do have these two tickets for the theater this evening..."

"Oh! Oh, gee...I don't think..."

He raised a hand, stopping her protest. "Yes, yes, I know. *Charlotte*. Well, forget Charlotte. She's going to be in bed the rest of the evening. Besides, she'll understand. It just seems a shame to throw away a pair of hundred-dollar tickets. What do you say? Can you get dressed in time?" He paused, his eyes taking in her less-than-elegant ensemble. "Did you bring anything else?

To hell with Charlotte. Someone's offering you a free ticket to a Broadway show.

She laughed. "I never go anywhere without at least one respectable outfit." His smile told her the issue was settled. "Oh, all right," she said, pulling herself off of the sofa and starting toward the hall. "You talked me into it. I'll be back in five minutes."

"Five?" came the leery response.

"You're right. I do have to comb my hair. Make it ten."

"Damn."

Having reached the hallway, she turned back. "Seven?"

"What? Oh, no, it's not that...it's just that we can make the show without any problem, but we don't have enough time for dinner."

Brianna grinned. "I've got just the place."

They stood on the corner of 47th and Broadway, the pre-theater crowd swarming around them, while Brianna stared at her hot dog as if it were some sort of small, quick animal that she had to catch. She heard Spencer laugh.

"Nobody told you to put half the toppings in Times Square on the thing."

She sighed. "I know. I just couldn't decide what to have, so this is what I ended up with." Her first bite was anything but successful—most of the condiments landed on the sidewalk in front of her, causing more than one passerby to throw her a dirty look. If she hadn't bent over as quickly as she had, her light beige coat would have had an interesting multicolored decoration added to it.

"Good God, woman," Spencer shouted over the incessant traffic noise as he waved his own much more sedately embellished meal about for emphasis. "If you're going to order such a monstrosity, at least you should know how to get it into your mouth!"

She pretended to pout. "Be nice to me. I've never done this before." She rotated the hot dog in her hand, contemplating the best angle for attack. "Usually I limit myself to mustard. Or mustard and relish if I'm feeling particularly adventurous." One glance at Spencer's absurd expression and she started to laugh so hard she couldn't get the second bite, either, but then she took a deep breath, furrowed her brow in concentration and chomped down for all she was worth.

"Brava!" He pounded her on the back, nearly making her spill her soda.

Brianna grinned around a mouthful of relish and chili. "Oh, be quiet."

Spencer threw his waxed paper and soda can into a garbage basket with a hollow clatter as they walked. "Well, my dear, thanks to your inspired dinner plans, we've got a half hour before the show starts. Shall we go on to the theater?"

Brianna finished off her hot dog and shook her head. "Not yet. It's much more fun to watch all the weirdos, don't you think?" She wadded up her waxed paper into a neat little square and wiped her fingers on the harsh napkin she had picked up from the cart.

"Whatever the lady wishes." He made a little bow, then added with a wink, "Even if she is nuts."

They were having too good a time together, getting along too well, she thought with no small regret as they began a leisurely stroll through the bustling Broadway crowd. Being this comfortable with him made her wish that things could be different, and she didn't like that.

"Hey—" she said, trying to make her head change the subject, "that guy over there keeps staring at me. Do I have mustard on my face or something?" She tilted her face up to him.

"Here…let me see."

Taking his handkerchief out of his pocket, he tucked his fingers under her chin, having no idea of her reaction to the scorching warmth of his touch.

"Yes…there seems to be a bit of mustard…here…"

He gently wiped off a spot on the side of her mouth. His face was so close she could feel his breath. She started trembling, from the pit of her stomach to the ends of her limbs, hopeful and frightened and confused all at once. This wasn't what she expected, or wanted, or thought she'd ever feel.

This was no good.

"And a drop of relish, there…" The handkerchief dabbed at her chin, as the searing blue eyes inspected her face for other aberrations that might need to be remedied. "Okay. All done." The handkerchief and the warm hand were removed posthaste. "Now if someone ogles you, at least you can rest assured that your face is clean."

Trying to steady her breathing, Brianna jerked her head in the direction of a woman in four-inch heels, white leather miniskirt, and fake-leopard jacket, making rude kissing sounds in their direction, as she simultaneously jerked herself back to reality. "Gee—there's nothing on *your* face. Why do you suppose that woman is giving you the once-over?"

He grunted as they passed the bleached blonde, who clearly saw Brianna as no impediment to her plying her trade as she loudly suggested that Spencer would have a lot more fun with *her*.

As the woman's exaggerated moans of rejection trailed behind them, Brianna gasped when she caught sight of a bank clock up ahead. "Hey, wait a minute!" Brianna grabbed Spencer's wrist and jabbed a finger at his watch face. "Look—see that clock over there? Your watch is ten minutes slow!"

Without another word, he grabbed her by the elbow and pulled her through the crowd toward the theater, fishing for the tickets in his topcoat pocket as they ran. Breathless and laughing, they burst through the lobby doors as Spencer shoved the tickets at the bored-looking usher, who tore off the tops and gave the stubs back to him.

Of course, the seats were nearly in front, which meant a dash down a fifty-foot aisle, then plowing across a dozen or so sets of knees to their places. Without removing their coats, they plopped down into their seats just as the first notes of the overture floated out from the pit.

The urge to keep laughing threatened to overwhelm Brianna, made worse as she felt suspicious vibrations coming from the seat next to hers. Cautiously, she stole a glance at the side of Spencer's face, and saw that he was having the same problem.

She fell in love with him at that very moment, the moment when a fit of adolescent giggles threatened to dissolve the last vestige of the man's dignity. She had no idea what, if anything, she would or could do about it, but if nothing else, she could at least be honest with herself for the moment.

No matter how much the truth would probably hurt down the road.

Swallowing hard, she forced herself to keep her attention focused on the curtain three rows in front of them as she tried with only moderate success to keep her mirth in check. But then, nearly choking on his laughter, Spencer started to cough.

Brianna leaned over to him. "Do you need to get some water?" she whispered.

Spencer shook his head as he coughed even more loudly.

Brianna searched her purse for some mints. She finally found a half-consumed roll in one corner, covered with assorted unidentified bits of stuff. She couldn't offer them to a dog, much less a multimillionaire client.

And still he coughed.

Brianna felt a light tap on her arm, then noticed a package of cough drops in front of her, proffered by a very thin hand with platinum nails. She looked over, then down again, into a crumpled but fastidiously made-up face with a helmet of straw blond hair perched on top of it.

"Here. Take." The hand pushed the cough drops into Brianna's, then the face peered across her lap, then back up at Brianna. "What?" queried a Yiddish accent worthy of a vaudeville stage. "You couldn't get a *healthy* one?"

With that, Brianna's battle with her own giggles was irrevocably lost.

Engrossed in animated conversation, Brianna and Spencer spilled out onto the sidewalk after the show with the rest of the crowd, then stood like two rocks in a whitewater river as bodies flowed around them and off into the night.

Spencer didn't want the night to end, didn't want to face reality. If, indeed, he even knew yet what that was supposed to be. He touched Brianna's elbow and steered her down the street toward Broadway.

"Shall we get a cab back to the apartment?" he asked, raising his voice over the deafening roar of a subway train hurtling past underneath their feet, the rush of warm air from the grate billowing out the hem of Brianna's swing coat.

She shook her head as the rumble retreated. "I'd rather walk for a while, if that's all right."

He nodded toward her high heels. "Can you?"

Brianna laughed, and he thought what a wonderful sound that was. And what a dangerous thought *that* was.

"As long as I'm in no hurry," she was saying. Then, with a sigh, she looked around her. "I love New York at night. But whenever I come up here for Buyer's Week, I'm alone. I may be nuts, as you said, but I'm not stupid. I know better than to stroll along Broadway by myself after dark." Her smile was almost shy. "It's nice to have the company."

It was. They walked up Broadway in comfortable silence for several minutes, each with their hands in their pockets, idly inspecting offerings behind gated store windows or exchanging hushed surmising appraisals of this or that person they passed. When he was sure she wouldn't notice, Spencer regarded Brianna thoughtfully.

"You're not from Atlanta originally, are you?" he finally asked.

She shook her head, seeming to expect the question. "North Carolina. Greensboro. And then several years here in New York, which you know."

"And then?"

"And then I went back home to stay with my parents." She paused. "My mother was ill for a long time."

He glanced at the side of her face. "How is she now?"

"She died when I was twenty-five."

"Oh—I'm sorry."

She shrugged and hitched her shoulder bag up higher.

"And your father?"

"He died three years ago."

"Boy, I'm really batting a thousand tonight," he muttered. He felt her touch his sleeve.

"It's okay. Really."

The crease between her brows said otherwise, but he was hardly going to press the issue. Instead he asked, "So how did you end up in Atlanta?"

He watched the lines on her brow deepen as she clearly considered how much to say. Then, "Toss of the coin, really. My dad had been very frugal, which meant he stashed away or invested a good portion of his not-insubstantial earnings as a doctor. I was shocked, after his death, when the lawyer told me how much my inheritance was. I had no desire to stay in Greensboro, and really didn't want to live in New York, so I thought I'd try Atlanta. Then the opportunity came along with Luella's..." With a shrug, she finished. "And here I am."

"I take it you were an only child?"

"Yes. My parents were in their forties when I came along. I was their little spoiled brat."

He jerked toward her. "There's nothing spoiled about you, believe me."

A gust of steam floating out of a nearby manhole momentarily engulfed them as they turned off Broadway and began strolling east along Central Park South. "Oh, but I was, for a long time." She sighed. "I think I got it slapped out of me sometime in my twenties."

"Oh? How's that?"

"I'm not sure. I guess I just grew up. Learned there were smarter and more important people out there than I, that's all."

He smiled at her correct—but rarely heard—usage of the personal pronoun at the end of her sentence. "I doubt that there are many people who can even come close to you in the intelligence department, Brianna."

She turned to him with a half-smile. And a certain... *something* in her eyes he didn't want to see.

"Thank you," she said in that caressing voice of hers, and inside his head, everything went haywire.

The afterglow from his compliment didn't last long.

"But it's still incomprehensible to me," he slowly said, almost as if digging for the words, "how on earth you ended up in the bridal business. With your background and intelligence, I just think there're so many more...*worthwhile* things you could be doing."

She came to a halt, forcing him to stop, as well. Had she heard correctly? With a short laugh, she said, "I would very much appreciate it if you wouldn't make it sound as if I was running drugs, thank you very much." The buzz from the overhead street lamp filled the silence between them as Brianna watched Spencer's eyes glinting at her. With what she assumed was disapproval.

"You don't understand—" he started to say.

She was suddenly exhausted, and confused, and infuriated.

"No, Spencer—*you* don't understand," she said on a harsh sigh. "I thought we'd reached a truce about what I do, but suddenly I sense nearly as much antagonism about this as that first time you came to the salon. I don't like it, I don't understand it, and I really don't want to hear it anymore." She started to walk down the street, yanking her collar up around her neck.

"I'm sorry," Spencer said as he caught up to her. "I can't help what I feel. And I just think the whole wedding business is a big sham."

She whirled around. "Oh, you do? What about marriage itself? Do you think that's a waste of time, too?"

If he thought he was masking the struggle in his eyes, he was mistaken.

"If by that you mean some idealistic concept of two people being in love for the rest of their lives—pretty much."

For a moment disappointment supplanted anger, then she shrugged and resumed walking, telling herself she didn't care whether he followed or not. "Well, as much of the rest of the world does not feel the way you do," she snapped, "I happen to be filling a very real need."

"Brianna...I didn't mean to imply that I think that what you *do* is a waste of time...."

She turned on him, incredulous. "You just said as much not thirty seconds ago!" There was something in his face she couldn't read, something that went beyond his contempt for her profession. But he had to understand. She blew out an exasperated sigh. "Look, people are going to get married, whether you like it or not. And some of those people want big, fancy weddings. Like your mother and Colin's parents want for them, right? Well, putting on one of those big, fancy weddings is like putting on a Broadway show, with sets and props and costumes, and making sure the cast is where they're supposed to be when they're supposed to be there. That's what I do. I do it well, and people pay me well to do it. It's my *job*, Spencer." She stopped her tirade, then took a breath. "Nothing more."

His gaze in the half light was electrifying. "Why are you so defensive about this, Brianna?"

"*Me?* Why are *you?*" A siren wailed several blocks away, cutting them off. She lowered her head, waiting, but when no answer came from him, she said, "For one thing, you keep

her hysteria vanished as quickly as it had appeared, replaced by an eerie calmness. For several seconds, neither one of them spoke nor moved. Then Brianna finally said, her voice flat-sounding in her ears, "You have to admit, it's pretty ironic. The question is—do you *want* to marry Charlotte?"

With a sound somewhere between a snort and a laugh, Spencer replied, "The question is, as I'm sure you may have surmised, whether I wish to marry anyone."

After a long pause, Brianna whispered, "But what's the answer?"

When she realized he wouldn't—or couldn't—tell her what she already knew, she finally said with every scrap of graciousness she could muster, "Well. I hope you'll be very happy."

They rode up in the elevator together like strangers. Which, Spencer realized, they were, in spite of the fact that his lips still burned with the feel of hers. No other woman's kiss had had such an effect on him. Not even Charlotte's. Certainly not Charlotte's.

But one simply could not, did not, make decisions based on glandular disturbances, no matter how profound or disturbing. Or pleasant. Spencer made decisions based on logic, on facts, on solid reason.

Not on the memory of a pair of silken lips pressed against his.

And certainly not based on the tricks his heart tried to play on him. *That* he could never allow again. For most people, what the world called *love* was a cruel illusion, a concept trumped up by candy companies to sell more chocolate on Valentine's Day.

The elevator door opened. Brianna stepped out and stood stiffly by the door while he turned the key in the lock.

Charlotte stood in the center of the black-and-white-tiled vestibule, her arms tightly entwined against her ribs. She didn't speak; instead, her dark eyes glinted from his face to

Brianna's and back again and he could see she was trembling with anger.

And jealousy.

As if driven by some force he did not understand, Spencer crossed the space between them in two strides and took Charlotte in his arms. Seconds later, he heard Brianna's bedroom door slam shut.

Brianna leaned against the bedroom door, letting the tears stream unhindered down her cheeks. Almost unable to catch her breath, she pushed herself away and started to pace in front of the bed, clutching her folded arms to her chest, her tangled emotions once again raging in her head like a violent thunderstorm.

Well, lady, she thought as she snatched a tissue out of a box by the bed, *you certainly can't blame the man this time.* He could hardly be expected to drop his commitment to a woman he'd been dating for a year to pursue a relationship with someone he'd met four days ago, now could he? What did she expect, a profession of love after one kiss? Maybe she did see confusion in his eyes, hear ambivalence in his voice about this marriage. But that had nothing to do with *her.*

She wanted to throw something. Her glance flew around the room, lighting on the bed. Pillows. Tons of them. Feeling like a three-year-old having a wholloping good tantrum, she whipped pillow after pillow off the bed, hurling each one in turn with a resounding, satisfying *thwomp* at the upholstered armchair near the window.

The pillows now strewn across the room and the muscles in her left arm protesting, she slid down onto the floor with her back against the bed, wiping at her wet cheeks with the palm of her hand. Fat lot of good "admitting" that she loved Spencer did her now, huh? How could she have let her fantasies go that far? Was she really that naive?

Or…that desperate?

Her sobs eventually fading into sporadic hiccups, she sat immobile for several minutes, staring at the wainscoting on the side of the dresser. But it didn't matter, did it? What if there *had* been some indication that a relationship between them might blossom? What would *she* have been able to do about it? They were both adults, healthy adults, normal adults. Healthy, normal adults who…who love each other generally share more than a kiss or two, don't they?

Then what would she have done?

The hiccups finally stopped, as well, replaced by overwhelming exhaustion and frustration and helplessness as the last bit of adrenaline seeped from her bloodstream, leaving her numb.

There was no point in thinking about any of this anymore. Her limbs on automatic pilot, Brianna peeled off her clothes where she sat, then hauled herself off the floor and pulled her flannel nightgown out from under the pillow, dragging it down over her naked torso with great effort. Sniffling, she pulled back the covers and climbed into bed, grabbed another tissue from the box on the nightstand, and clicked off the bedside lamp. She blew her nose, gave a loud, shuddering sigh, and flopped onto her back, staring at the textured ceiling in the blue-gray moonlight.

As if reciting a calming mantra, she began to go over her schedule for the next day, what she and Kelly needed to accomplish before Brianna flew back to Atlanta. Her thoughts wandered into the next week, the next month. Suddenly she remembered she hadn't entered an appointment into her Day-timer. Knowing she'd forget it again if she didn't take care of it immediately, she forced herself to get out of bed and retrieve the book from her tote bag.

She sat down in front of a small desk in the room and clicked on the lamp, yawning as she flipped through the pages of the appointment book. She entered the notation she had remembered, then frowned, suddenly awake.

It's that time of month, Kelly had said at breakfast, *when I could eat half of New York.*

She scanned the previous month's entries, her eyes falling on a personal notation. Then she turned back to the current month, knowing what wasn't there, feeling the blood drain from her face.

A hollow, almost metallic-sounding laugh escaped her throat. Oh, how proud she'd always been of her ability to uncomplicate the basically messy business of being a human being, simply by being so organized, controlled, focused. Now, with one slip of judgment, it had all just gone sailing out the window. Allowing herself to fall in love with Spencer Lockhart was *nothing* compared with this.

She counted backward, aloud, as if hearing herself would make it more real.

Her last period had been six weeks ago.

...

5

"**Y**ou're a damned fool, Spencer."

Spencer regarded his handsome mother's stony expression across the breakfast table with a wry smile. "I believe the correct thing to say at times like this is *Congratulations. I hope you'll be very happy.*"

Edwina Lockhart sniffed, then fixed her chalky blue eyes on her son. "I kept my mouth shut about dating her, figuring you'd come to your senses sooner or later. Obviously I was wrong." She shook her head, her gray waves glinting in a patch of morning sun. "Maybe I should just go on back to Europe. It'd be easy enough. My bags are still packed."

Spencer chuckled and poured himself another cup of coffee. In spite of his mother's imposing physical presence—she was nearly six feet tall, and age had made her voice almost as deep as his—he had never been intimidated by her.

"You're not going anywhere, Mother, and you know it." He stirred his coffee, then set the spoon on his saucer with a soft *clink*. "You really don't know Charlotte, you know. Have you even exchanged more than ten words with her?"

"I don't have to talk to the girl to know she's not right for you." Edwina squinted at her son. "Or to know that you don't love her."

Spencer sighed. "Love her?" With a shrug, he added, "I care for her, certainly. You know my opinion on romantic love." Knowing that he dare not let himself be trapped by his mother's eyes, he shifted his attention toward the window.

"Charlotte will be a good wife. And maybe I'll get that grand-child for you you've always wanted."

"No one wants a grandchild that badly." She swallowed the bite of cereal in her mouth and shook her head. "For that matter, I didn't think you were all that hot on the idea of children."

Spencer chuckled and looked back at his mother. "I have to admit, that one even took me by surprise." He shrugged. "But I suddenly realized I was seeing other people's kids and wondering what it would be like to have one of my own. It took its sweet time, but I guess the old urge to procreate finally kicked in." On a sigh, he added, "I'm really ready to be a father. What can I tell you?"

He didn't flinch as his mother silently scrutinized him for several seconds. Then she stood and stacked her own breakfast dishes to take them into the kitchen, just as she always did. As far back as Spencer could remember, his mother had been adamant that the servants were there to do what she *couldn't* do, not what she *could*. Balancing her cup, saucer, and cereal bowl in her hands, she shook her head. "Something's going on that you're not telling. If, in fact, you even know what the hell it is yourself. You never even hinted that you might ask this girl to marry you. Now, suddenly, the wedding's in three months?" She narrowed her eyes again. "She pregnant?"

"No, Mother."

"You're sure?"

He laughed. "Yes, I'm sure." As it had been quite some time since he and Charlotte had been intimate, it was a moot point. "Her daddy's not coming after me with a shotgun, be-lieve me. Besides, I'd hardly wait another three months, if that were the case." He took a last swallow of coffee and changed the subject. "I think you'll like…Miss Fairchild," he called to his mother as she carried her dishes out to the kitchen, then returned. "She's got a good head on her shoulders."

"Glad to hear *somebody* does around here," Mrs. Lockhart muttered as she swept some crumbs off the table into the palm of her hand. She looked up. "When's she coming?"

"By nine. Any minute."

"Good. Maybe talking about your sister's wedding will get my mind off *yours*."

That last day in New York had felt like a bad dream. Between the discovery of her late period and Spencer's cold announcement to her that morning of his engagement to Charlotte, Brianna's only wish had been that the day would be over as quickly as possible. Once through with her meeting with Kelly—an appointment she had admittedly rushed through—she spent the rest of the day by herself museum-hopping, unable to shake the nagging depression that clung to her like an overgrown vine.

In spite of her situation, her spirits had lifted somewhat once back in Atlanta, in large part due to a hectic schedule since her return that had simply left her little time to worry about her predicament, even though she knew she'd have to deal with it soon. Very soon.

Dr. Steinberg had been very sympathetic. And concerned.

"I thought you'd told me that you weren't sexually active?" the gray-haired woman had asked, nearly as shocked as Brianna at the positive pregnancy test.

Brianna had given a short laugh. "I wasn't, when I last came in." She sighed. "And I'm not now."

"So…the father's out of the picture?"

"You could say that."

"Why didn't he use a condom?"

Brianna had flushed to the roots of her hair. "He'd said he'd had a vasectomy…"

With a sigh, the doctor scanned her chart. "Well, at least, everything checks out with the blood tests."

"Excuse me?"

"There are no STDs." The doctor searched Brianna's face with a grim set to her mouth. "Sexually transmitted diseases?"

"Oh…"

"You're very lucky, Brianna. You should have used protection in any case, no matter what he told you."

She had felt overwhelmingly stupid. But Dr. Steinberg hadn't meant to chastise her. Exactly. The doctor raised her chin to look at her through her bifocals.

"Well, dear...what do you want to do?"

Brianna knew what she was asking. But she'd already made a decision. Even though her insides had been shaking with sheer terror, she'd smiled and announced, "I'm going to have a *baby,* doctor." And then she'd burst into tears.

And the doctor had just nodded as she patted her hand, reminded her about fluctuating hormones and mood swings, and scheduled Brianna's next prenatal appointment.

That had been two weeks ago. Now, she was due out at the Lockhart estate in an hour. She wearily climbed into her minivan, latched the seat belt, started the car, pulled out of her driveway.

I'm going to have a baby.

The thought had crossed her mind a thousand times since coming home. And each time it did, it sounded a little more real. And a little less daunting.

In spite of the fact that she would be doing this entirely on her own, in spite of the fact that this child was not conceived in love—or even, she thought wryly, in pleasure—as the fetus inside her grew, so did her satisfaction with the idea. At thirty-three, she had almost reconciled herself to the fact that she might never have children. Now, every time she saw a baby being pushed along in a stroller or nestled in a Snugli carrier or toddling along on its mother's hand, she felt a surge of excitement like nothing she'd ever felt before.

It helped to temper the nausea, which this morning could only be described as excruciating.

She headed straight out Peachtree Road up into Buckhead, glancing periodically at the map that Spencer had faxed her the day before, then began the meandering path that would lead to the Lockhart estate. She came to a stop sign and picked up the map, then checked the street sign as the magnificent houses all around her seemed to watch her, awaiting her decision.

The last turn? Yes.

She drove for a few more minutes, her mind blank, until she came to a set of ten-foot-high gates. The gatekeeper buzzed her in and she found herself on a winding road with nothing but woods on either side of her. Another time, she might have enjoyed the pretty drive, but another wave of sickness threatened to pull her under as she flipped down the visor to shield her eyes from the sun splintering through the bare-branched trees. She hadn't actually thrown up that morning, but all bets were off as to whether she'd make it through the day without facing the inside of a toilet bowl.

She pulled the van up into what was, for all intents and purposes, a small parking lot on the side of the house. As she got out of the car, she saw Spencer walking down the gravel drive toward her, more austere than ever in a charcoal double-breasted suit with a blue shirt nearly the same color as his eyes. Her stomach pitched again. For some reason, she had assumed that he wouldn't be there.

"Good morning, Miss Fairchild."

She forced herself to smile and returned the salutation in kind, acutely aware of their return to formality. "Mr. Lockhart." The nausea was merciless. She felt a cold sweat begin to seep from her brow. "I saw...the announcement in Sunday's paper," she said, unconsciously placing her hand on her throat and tugging at the collar of her cream silk blouse.

"Yes. Charlotte hated her photo." He didn't sound any more enthusiastic today than he had when he'd first told her of the engagement. He paused, watching her, his breath hovering in puffs of moisture in front of his face in the early spring morning air. "I never asked you...but I...*we* were wondering if you'd handle the wedding for us— Oh, Lord! Are you all right?"

A dizzy spell had forced her to lean against the side of the car, her pale peach wool suit an immediate victim of her distress. She tried to nod, but the bile in her throat would not let her lie. "I…just don't feel very well this morning…."

Frowning, Spencer immediately put his arm around her and led her toward the house. "Good God, woman—I've seen roadkill that looked better than you do. Are you coming down with the flu?"

She shrugged, then swallowed as hard as she could, fighting to keep everything under control until they reached the house, feeling her knees growing weaker by the second. The instant they were through the door, however, she said in a voice no louder than a squeak, "Do you think it might be possible for me to use your rest room?"

She *felt* much better after throwing up, but she certainly didn't *look* any better. Her hands braced on either side of the marble powder room sink, she stared at her reflection in the mirror, wondering who this pale, sunken-cheeked woman with the ghastly circles under her eyes could possibly be. Certainly not her. *She.* Whatever. Trying to keep her hands steady, she fished some blush and lipstick out of her handbag and attempted to fix herself up before she frightened somebody. If she hadn't already. Spencer had looked truly horror-stricken a few minutes ago.

She managed to remove most of the car dirt from her jacket sleeve; then, wobbly-kneed but otherwise pulled together, she emerged from the powder room to be met by a statuesque older woman casually clad in a rose velour running suit. Her short hair was the color of old pewter, and her pale blue eyes, which emanated kindness and concern, were framed by arched charcoal brows.

"Are you all right now, honey?" the woman asked in a voice that was very Southern and very gracious. Like Spencer had five minutes before, she immediately looped a steady arm around Brianna's waist.

Brianna nodded and gave her a weak smile. "Not the most auspicious way to visit someone's home for the first time."

The woman waved her hand and laughed, her voice a lower

timbre than most men's. "Oh, now, don't you think another thing about it, Miss Fairchild," she said, guiding her toward a doorway a few feet away. "I'm Edwina Lockhart, by the way, if you hadn't already figured that out."

"I had, in fact." Brianna ventured a more secure smile, beginning to feel less like a candidate for the morgue.

"Let's sit and chat for a bit before we tour the house. You don't look any too steady on those thin legs of yours yet." Mrs. Lockhart led Brianna into what she assumed was the library. A pair of shelved walls overflowed with books of every size, while the two flanking walls were the yellow of daffodils. Three stately multipaned windows stood guard on one end of the room, on one seat of which lay an overblown white Persian cat with eyes the same vivid blue, Brianna realized with an inward smile, as Spencer's.

"Sit," Spencer's mother gently commanded, waving a large, blue-veined hand toward one of a pair of white leather sofas. "Feel up to a cup of tea?"

Brianna sighed as she sank into a cloud of down. "That would be lovely. Thank you." She watched as Mrs. Lockhart spoke into an intercom placed on the wall, then sat opposite her.

"Spencer's making some calls in the other room, in case you're wondering where he's gone off to. He'll be in later. Says you're going to handle *his* wedding, too."

She felt herself blush under the trenchant blue gaze. "Actually, I hadn't had a chance to discuss it with him...." Brianna lowered her eyes to her hands, realizing they were clasped together in her lap like a Chinese puzzle. The nausea tried to resurface. She changed the subject. With a smile, she said, "I was a little worried about accommodating such a large wedding in a private home. I see my fears were ungrounded."

Mrs. Lockhart just smiled and crossed her long legs, clearly deciding to follow the conversational path Brianna had chosen. "And you've only seen this room and the downstairs bath! I believe the square footage of the house is in the neighborhood of twenty-thousand."

"Even so—I don't imagine you're planning on trying to seat a thousand people inside somewhere?"

The older woman gave a great, deep laugh. "Oh, my Lord, honey, no! That's why God gave us gardens! As long as He gives us a sunny day, as well, we'll be in business."

"Unfortunately, *that* I can't promise. Tents are fine for little rain showers, but if it's a downpour..." Brianna smiled. "We'll need a contingency."

Mrs. Lockhart nodded. "I think we've pretty much decided to keep the wedding itself limited to family and a few close friends. No more than two hundred or so. There's a ballroom that should accommodate that number with no problem, I think you'll see. The rest of the crowd can come for the reception, which is all they want to do anyway!" She bellowed. "And if it rains, we can just stuff 'em in various rooms throughout the house."

Brianna chuckled. "Sounds like a good plan to me."

An unobtrusive maid came in with the tea, set it down on the wrought-iron and smoked-glass coffee table in front of Mrs. Lockhart, then left. Brianna realized that she was being studied again. Unembarrassed, she asked, "What is it, Mrs. Lockhart?"

The older woman shook her head and sighed. "Oh, nothing. And please call me Edwina. When you get old, the mind takes off in its own directions." She leaned forward and poured out two cups of tea.

"Trust me," Brianna said with a laugh. "Age has nothing to do with it. I do that all the time."

Edwina flashed her a warm smile, then asked, "Sugar or milk?"

"Both, please, thank you."

Spencer's mother handed Brianna her tea. "And what did you think of my little girl?"

"Oh, Kelly's lovely. I can't wait for her to see my preliminary sketches for her dress."

The blue eyes lit up. "Did you bring 'em with you?"

"Ah...no. Kelly made me swear that I wouldn't show them to anyone else until she gives her approval."

Mrs. Lockhart took a sip of her tea. "You're absolutely right. The last thing Kelly needs is her old momma butting her nose in." Settling into the corner of the sofa, she asked, "I suppose she told you she doesn't want the big wedding?"

There was no point in evading the issue. "She did."

"And what did you say?"

"That I'd make it as painless for her as possible." Brianna shrugged, then smiled. "I'm hardly likely to talk myself out of a job, am I?"

Spencer's mother sized up Brianna for a long moment, then hooted with laughter again. "Now I see what Spencer was talking about... And here he is, speak of the devil. Oh...but do you feel up to walking around yet, Miss Fairchild?"

"Yes," Brianna quickly replied, keeping her eyes on her hostess. "I'm fine now." *What Spencer was talking about?* Willing herself to forget the older woman's comment about her son, she pushed herself off of the sofa, wryly noting that such activity would, in all likelihood, become increasingly difficult over the next several months.

Spencer's mother had insisted he show her the house and grounds by himself, saying she had several calls to make. There was no way Brianna could object and not arouse suspicion. But now the air hung thickly between them as they walked, in spite of their best efforts to keep the conversation natural.

"Your home is incredible," she said at last, the awe in her voice unfeigned. "It's one of the prettiest homes I've ever seen. Even for Buckhead."

He cast a brief look in her direction, then nodded. "Thank you. Though I can't take any of the credit. Kelly and I are the third generation to live in the house."

They were standing in the middle of one of the formal gardens; she nodded toward a flat grassy area to the east. "I'd like to set up the tents over there." She turned to Spencer, *making* me defend myself. And for another…'' She squeezed shut her eyes and spilled out, before she remembered the dozen reasons why she shouldn't, ''Because I very much want you to approve of what I do.'' She lifted her face to his, and swallowed. Hard. ''To approve of *me*.''

She could not recall when he took her by the shoulders, when his firm, warm mouth had crushed hers in a desperate kiss that obliterated every bit of the rage. It happened so fast that she didn't even have time to fully realize what *was* happening, let alone be afraid. When he pushed himself away, his face was contorted in anguish.

''Oh, God…I'm so sorry, Brianna. That was really stupid of me…''

Her lips tingled, still aware of his. She reached up to touch his cheek, but he pulled away. ''Spencer…there's nothing to be sorry about…''

''No?'' The word tore from his throat. ''Well, there sure will be tomorrow.''

A nagging dull pain began to swell in the pit of her stomach. ''I don't understand….''

''Charlotte wants to get married.''

She couldn't move or think or speak for what seemed like several minutes. And then a torrent of emotions rushed through her brain, fomenting a wild, irrational laughter that bubbled up from the bottom of her stomach. *You couldn't allow me even ten seconds to be happy,* she thought as she listened to the unpleasant, choking sounds coming from her own throat. *Not even ten lousy seconds.* Her knees sagged with the weight of the pain, of the laughter, and she leaned against the Plexiglas wall of a bus stop, clutching her sides.

''I bet *that* went over well,'' she said, her voice way too high, aware of her near hysteria as she saw Spencer's appropriately odd expression. ''I mean, think about it. Wasn't it just two minutes ago that I heard you say, very clearly, that you thought marriage was a sham? Or was that someone else who just looked like you?''

Then he turned away, his mouth drawn into a tight line, and

pushing back a strand of hair that a breeze had blown across her face. "What do you think?"

He must have been watching her, because he precipitously looked away, jiggling a set of keys in his pocket. The lines on either side of his tightly set mouth seemed to be more deeply etched this morning. "You have carte blanche to do whatever you want. You know that."

"I know... I just wanted your opinion."

He glanced at her, unsmiling. "But I don't have one. It's not my wedding."

She nodded, ignoring the pain in her heart, in his eyes. "No." With a short intake of breath, she asked, "But what about yours? Are you planning on holding it here, as well?"

"So. You *will* do it."

"If you like," she replied, wondering how she managed to keep her voice steady.

He paused, then said in a low voice, "Well, then, I can assure you that Charlotte would rather die than have *her* wedding even remotely resemble my sister's. Believe me, she'll want something completely different."

"I can understand that," Brianna said. "I probably would be the same way, in the same circumstances," she added, kicking at a small stone with the tip of her shoe.

They walked in silence for a minute or so. Brianna had begun to come to terms with the constant ache in the middle of her chest whenever she saw, or even thought about, Spencer. Even if there had been no Charlotte, there would have been no way the relationship could have worked now. That was a foregone conclusion the moment she discovered her pregnancy. But wasn't the dual impediment of Charlotte and the pregnancy just as well, under the circumstances? What kind of relationship could she possibly have, anyway?

And why couldn't she just accept the situation and forget about it?

Forget about *him?*

Like someone obsessed with digging out a splinter in spite of the pain it causes, she returned the conversation to his plans.

Maybe if she kept talking about it, it would stop hurting so much.

"Charlotte really needs to come see me about her gown as soon as possible, you know. Whether I design it or we order it from somewhere, it still takes about eight weeks."

He stopped walking and squinted off into the distance. "Yes, of course. I'll tell her to call you."

Brianna took a deep breath, no longer able to tolerate the aloofness she heard in his voice whenever he spoke of his impending marriage. "Spencer—why are you marrying Charlotte?"

He whipped his head around, glaring at her with such intensity that she took a small step backward.

"And what the *hell* business is that of yours?"

She squared her shoulders and met his stare, ignoring her trembling knees. "None, I admit. Except..." Blinking back tears, she said on a sigh, "It hurts me to see you like this."

The blue eyes darted away like a spooked animal's. Feeling that she had nothing more to lose, Brianna persisted, "Three weeks ago, you made it very clear that you'd rather wrestle snakes than get married. And now you are. Getting married." She sighed. "You've asked me to handle the affair. I'm not really comfortable working on a wedding where one of the major participants seems so ambivalent about the whole thing—"

"Please..." His expression was harder than she'd ever seen it. "You don't expect me to believe that, do you? None of your clients has ever had prewedding jitters?"

Suddenly weary, Brianna sat on a stone bench, her hands dropping helplessly into her lap. "Of course they have. But that's not what's going on here and you know it." She could hardly feel herself breathe and her heart was ramming against her rib cage, but she managed to say, "It's pretty obvious you're about to marry a woman you don't love."

Spencer had remained standing, his gaze fixed on some point a hundred, two hundred, feet away. A pure white butterfly danced on the breeze in front of them, fragile and innocent. "And what do you know about love, Miss Fairchild?" Spencer asked at last, his voice quiet. Brittle.

"More than you might think," she rejoined, not caring how he read her message. He shut his eyes; she watched the muscles in his jaw working overtime. "It just seems to me that *love* would be the only reason that you *would* marry. This just doesn't make sense, that's all."

Several seconds passed. When he at last spoke, the words came in a monotone. "I'll be away for the next six weeks in Japan. You can deal with Kelly herself or my mother in my absence."

Their conversation had been filed away in a back drawer of his mind like some unwanted business solicitation. "Oh... I see." Brianna stood, straightening out her skirt. "That's...fine." She started back toward the house, speaking in an even tone to match his. "I'll draw up some plans and get them to your mother, then."

She had risen too quickly, becoming dizzy after walking a few feet. Reaching out to steady herself on a stone pillar by the path, all the emotions she'd tried to keep under such a tight rein broke loose. Even though the light-headedness quickly passed, she hoped unnoticed, her entire body now shook as if beset by a virulent illness.

"And please tell Charlotte to contact me...as soon as possible so we can get started..."

Pushing herself away from the pillar, she quickly distanced herself from Spencer, wanting to reach the house, to collect her things, to leave. But the landscape started to undulate under her feet, the path in front of her weaving viciously in and out of the dancing topiaries. She stumbled, clutched at air, felt Spencer's arms pull her to safety.

"Oh, Brianna..."

Please, she thought, hearing her heart pound in her ears. *Not the kindness. I can't deal with the kindness.* She gulped for breath and willed her head to clear. With strength she wasn't sure she had, she dug the heels of her hands into his chest and pushed him away.

"*No!*"

She searched his anguished eyes for only a second, then wheeled around and strode back to the house, praying for all she was worth that he would have at least enough sense not to follow her.

Feeling suffocated by his own stupidity, Spencer stared out the library window, watching Brianna's van drive away.

"She's a big girl, honey," his mother assured him, touching his arm. "Just leave her be."

He tried to sound no more concerned than anyone else might be. "Maybe. But she's clearly not well. What if she has one of those dizzy spells again in the middle of traffic?"

"Spence—what happened in the garden?"

He glanced at her, then away. "Nothing." He heard his mother's snort beside him.

"You do realize, don't you, that you look far worse than she did?"

"She…gave me a fright, that's all," Spencer replied in a level voice. "I'm not used to having ladies go chalk white and swoon in front of me."

"No, I suppose not." Edwina leaned back against the top of one of the sofas and crossed her arms. "You're not handling this very well, you know."

"I have no idea what you're talking about, Mother."

"Yes, you do," she said quietly. "You're marrying the wrong girl."

He covered up for the lump in his throat with a short cough, finally meeting his mother's cool gaze five feet away. "Don't be ridiculous. Charlotte will make a perfect wife."

"So you said."

They remained eye to eye for several seconds, Spencer unnerved by the strange expression in his mother's steely eyes. At last she raised her hands in surrender and said, "Fine. Believe whatever makes you happy." She stood and patted his back, her tone changed. "Miss Fairchild'll be *fine,* son. Quit fretting so much. It makes your face all pinched. Now—are you going into work today or not?''

"Yes." His answer was as short as his temper. "I've got a helluva lot to clear up before I leave for Tokyo." He crossed the room and picked up his briefcase. "Listen, I'm going to tell Charlotte to get in touch with Br—Miss Fairchild about her gown. Apparently it takes eight weeks just to get a dress." He paused. "Would you just keep an eye out while I'm gone?''

Edwina arched an eyebrow. "Keep an eye out on *whom?*"

Spencer looked down at his briefcase for a moment. "Just *things,* Mother. Just keep an eye on things for me." He hesitated, then said, "Charlotte can be a lot to handle, if you don't know how. I just don't...want her bullying Miss Fairchild too much, that's all.''

Edwina chuckled.

"What's so funny?"

"Do you really think that young woman is going to let the likes of Charlotte Westwood ruffle her feathers?''

Spencer thought for a moment, then one side of his mouth hitched up as he remembered his face-offs with Brianna a few weeks ago. "No, probably not." He started to leave.

"Spencer?"

He was halfway across the library, but pivoted back to his mother, dreading what the tone of her voice foretold.

"Yes?"

She tilted her head, studying his face with her characteristic squint. "This is your mother you're talking to, remember? You never could lie about diddly to me, 'cause I could always read your face like a book. So let me just say that if you're trying to convince me that your feelings for Miss Fairchild are only platonic, you're an even worse liar than I'd thought.''

Spencer rubbed the back of his neck, wishing like hell his mother did not have such a knack for zeroing in on his thoughts. But she was not a nag. Once she'd voiced her opinion, she wouldn't harp on it. If he kept his thoughts to himself, the subject would never come up again.

At least, not in so many words.

"It's just that Miss Fairchild has no one else," he said at last. "No family, no real friends that I can tell. She'd never admit it, but I think she's a very lonely lady."

Edwina crossed to where the mammoth feline lay, scooping him up into her arms. "I figured as much. Though why such a lovely young woman should be all alone is beyond me." She hesitated, gazing out through the window over the east garden as she stroked the arrogant animal's head. "You were right, by the way."

"About what?"

The cat squirmed out of her arms when she faced him. "About her. Miss Fairchild. I liked her *very* much. And she does have a good head on her shoulders." She grinned. "A very *pretty* head, I might add."

There wasn't a damn thing he could say to that.

Spencer sat back in the leather swivel chair behind his desk with his hands locked behind his head and let out a stream of air through his lips. Thank God his conversation with Charlotte had been as brief as it had been. His needing to be away for six weeks had not gone down well with his fiancée. He was loathe to admit it, but ever since they'd become engaged, she'd been whiny and demanding and generally a pain in the butt. Wedding nerves, he guessed. *Hoped.* At least he'd gotten her to promise to call Fairchild's right away and set up her first appointment.

He checked his watch. Amazingly enough, he'd gotten everything more or less straightened out with an hour yet before he had to leave for the airport. After a spine-popping stretch, he got out of the chair and walked over to the bar with the full intention of concocting a very dry martini. Once there, however, he lost interest. He chuckled to himself as he replaced the gin bottle. Then he caught a glimpse of himself in

the mirror over the bar, saw the harrowed expression in his
own eyes.

He thought of Brianna's frightened expression a few hours
ago in the garden, how her eyes had pleaded with his not to…

Not to what?

Changing his mind once more, he fixed himself the drink.

Whether he liked it or not, his mother was right. He was
not handling any of this very well. Oh, Charlotte would make
a suitable enough wife, but, as everyone kept reminding him,
he didn't love her. And never would, not the way people usually thought about love. Of course, up until a couple of weeks
ago, he didn't think he was capable of loving *anyone*.

The thought had slipped into his mind like an unwanted
piece of mail. Was he *in love* with Brianna Fairchild? Was
that why her beautiful face—not Charlotte's!—kept cropping
up in his thoughts? Why he ached to touch her, to take her in
his arms and tell her she would never be alone again? *You
don't believe in love, remember?* He left his drink half finished
and returned to his desk. *And certainly not love at first sight.*

But that's exactly what it had been, hadn't it?

No!

Yes.

Brianna Fairchild was an irresistible blend of elegance and
fire, unaffected charm and sheer guts. Then she'd thrown in
disarming honesty and a wry sense of humor—good God! He
sucked in his breath: he'd never stood a chance.

He willed his hands to fill his briefcase with files he'd need
for the trip, shaking his head vigorously in a futile gesture of
denial. Damn! What an *idiot* he was, letting himself be talked
into marriage to one woman when his heart, his soul, was
being drawn to another. But how could he turn his back on a
woman he'd been involved with for the better part of a year?
If nothing else, he'd always thought of himself as a man of
honor. He did not break promises, written or implied, in his
personal affairs anymore than he did in his business dealings.

But, it occurred to him as his hands stopped their busywork, he had never promised Charlotte anything beyond treating her with respect and consideration, which he always had. Marriage had been *her* idea.

He slumped down into his desk chair, cupping his face in his hands.

So...why *had* he agreed to marry Charlotte?

Because, came the nagging little voice, *Brianna Fairchild can't get to you if you're married to someone else.*

A rattling sigh shook from his throat, as if he'd just uncovered a long-embedded thorn.

But she *had* gotten to him. Badly.

"I don't want to be in love! Do you hear?" he shouted to the air as his fist crashed onto the top of his desk.

Falling in love. Even the expression itself sounded unstable, off balance. And if there was one thing Spencer Lockhart could not abide, it was feeling out of control. With Charlotte, he was in command of the situation.

But with Brianna, it was like diving into a lake with no bottom. No matter how enticing the water might be, it was dangerous, because there was no way to get your footing. You could drown.

Or you could relax and float.

He slammed shut his briefcase, wishing he could shut up his muddled thoughts the same way. *See?* he chided himself as he jerked his briefcase off the desk and crossed to the closet, dropping the case into a nearby chair. See what all this nonsense about love, and romance, and marriage led to? It had turned a grown man, the head of a multibillion-dollar business empire, into a petulant child. He wrenched his coat off the hanger so hard it spun around the rod and flew out of the closet, nearly hitting him in the face.

A petulant child who didn't have a clue what to do about it.

He yanked on his topcoat, muttering to himself. Thank God

for this trip to Japan, giving him time away from Brianna. Out of sight, out of mind. As for Charlotte, perhaps absence would make the heart grow fonder. But not *too* fond.

God help him if he got the two mixed up while he was away.

6

Zoe stuck her head into Brianna's office. "You've got to come see Clarice in her suit. What a knockout!"

"Oh, yeah? Okay, I'll be right there."

After Zoe left, Brianna munched down another saltine and grimaced. If she never saw another cracker again, it would be too soon. But she still wasn't quite over the bouts of the woozies, and the stupid things did seem to help. At least, she could enjoy smells again without becoming ill, she thought as the sweet fragrance of lilacs wafted through the open window.

She brushed off a few crumbs from her blouse and went into the fitting room. Brianna smiled broadly the instant she saw the bride, who had been her accountant since she bought the business.

"Brother! Zoe wasn't kidding. You're gonna knock 'em dead."

Clarice grinned back, her pearl-like teeth a gleaming contrast to her bronze skin. "Yeah, not bad, huh?" She ran a set of brick red fingernails down the front of the fitted white satin jacket with bugle-beaded lapels, its long peplum flaring out over a slim, floor-length skirt. "And everyone thinks I'm just some old dull CPA!" Turning back to the mirror, she frowned. "What do you think about the headpiece, though?"

"What's to think?" Brianna replied with a quick shrug. "It's perfect."

"I guess you're right." Clarice sighed as she touched the small beaded satin cap hugging her head, from which a froth of veil exploded to her elbows. She mugged at herself in the mirror. "I do look good, don't I?" With a laugh, she added, "Now I don't want to take it off."

"So don't. It's paid for, you can do whatever you want with it. But I have to warn you—after two weeks, the novelty will have worn off."

"Good point." As the accountant removed her outfit, she said, "So...I see you're doing the Lockhart-Westwood wedding. That ought to build up the old coffers nicely."

Brianna ignored the ache in the middle of her chest as she hung up Clarice's wedding suit. "Yes...it should be quite an affair. *If* I can ever get the bride to decide on anything." She leaned back against the arm of one of the chairs in the fitting room and crossed her arms.

"Has she even chosen her dress?" Clarice asked as she slipped on her blouse.

"Uh-uh. She doesn't want me to design anything for her because, frankly, a Fairchild original isn't what she has in mind." Brianna didn't even attempt to disguise the distaste in her voice. After two weeks of trying to work with Charlotte Westwood, Brianna could say in all honesty that she did not like Spencer's bride-to-be. At all.

"Oh, give me a break! You're kidding, right?"

With a sigh, Brianna shook her head. "Wish I was. Anyway, I told her I could get in nearly anything she saw in a magazine. So what does she do? She brings in last month's *Town and Country* and shows me a photo of some twenty-thousand-dollar ballgown, says *this* is the dress she wants."

"Oh, jeez." Clarice let out a disgusted laugh as she buttoned up her blouse, then tucked it into her skirt. "So what did you do?"

"I think just maybe I can get the gown for her, but, brother—the phone calls and faxes I've had to make!"

"Well, all I have to say is, better you than me." She slipped on her jacket, pulling out the collar over the lapels. "How's the groom holding up through all of this?"

Brianna somehow managed to keep her smile in place. "He took the easy way out and went to Japan for six weeks."

"Yeah, I bet I know a certain man in my life who'd like to be in Japan right about now. Hell, he'd settle for *Siberia!*" Clarice laughed as she stepped into her patent leather pumps. "Okay, Miss Wedding Lady—am I done?"

Brianna stood and checked the bride's folder. "Yep. We'll schedule a final fitting for three days before in case you decide to gain ten pounds between now and your wedding, but other than that, that's it."

Placing her hand on her stomach, Clarice sighed. "I think it's more likely that I'll *lose* ten pounds than gain it. Getting married right after tax season? I must have been plumb out of my ever-loving mind!" She walked to the door of the dressing room, then backtracked. "Did you get everything straightened out with the florist?"

With an indulgent smile, Brianna nodded. "And the caterer. And the photographer." She gave her accountant a gentle nudge out the door. "Go back to work. Forget about your wedding. Forget about everything. Just say to yourself, as many times a day as it takes, 'It's all under control, it's all under control.' Okay?"

"Humph. That's easy for *you* to say. It ain't your wedding, child!"

They had made it as far as the hallway. Zoe intercepted them with a pained expression plastered across her face. "She's *he*-re..."

Clarice raised her eyebrows at Brianna. "Let me guess. Charlotte Westwood."

"Not just Charlotte," Zoe interjected. "Her *mother* is with her."

Brianna sighed and put her hand on Clarice's arm. "For your own safety, I suggest you evacuate now."

"Oh, it can't be that bad...."

"Oh, yes it can," Zoe said, rolling her black eyes. "If Attila the Hun had a mother, *this* is what she must have been like."

Zoe saw Clarice to the door as Brianna, smiling her

sweetest, greeted Charlotte and her mother. The sessions had
been difficult enough when just Charlotte was present; when
her mother was there, they became nightmarish.

Mrs. Westwood was no more than an older, wider version
of Charlotte, her figure strangled at the waist by a merry
widow corset that only served to redistribute sagging flesh to
other areas of her body, particularly her bottom. Brianna sometimes feared that the woman would become permanently
wedged into one of the salon's Bergere chairs. Her skin had
been pulled taut by so many face-lifts that she always appeared
slightly startled, no matter what the conversation. Like Charlotte, her makeup was always precision-perfect, but whereas
on the twenty-something Charlotte, the contrast between her
dark red lips and fair skin was striking, on the older woman
it just looked macabre.

"Well! It's about *time,* Miss Fayuhchild," Mrs. Westwood
drawled, the red lips pulled into a grotesque smile. "Now, you
know it's bad mannuhs to keep a client *waitin',* honey."

Brianna felt the beginning of a headache pull at the muscles
at the nape of her neck. "I'm *so* sorry, Mrs. Westwood, Miss
Westwood…" She acknowledged Charlotte with a brief nod.
"But I was with another bride. Besides—" Brianna nodded
toward the mantel clock "—you're early. Your appointment
isn't until one-thirty."

"Did you make *any* progress on getting that gown for me?"
Charlotte interrupted, not bothering to acknowledge Brianna
as she studied a handful of deep rose fingernails.

Brianna lifted her hand toward the conference room. "Let's
go in where we can be more comfortable, shall we?"

Zoe shot Brianna a glance of commiseration as she passed
her with the two ladies in tow. As she steered them into the
room, she answered Charlotte with a tight smile. "Yes, I received a fax from Paris yesterday, in fact. If we order within
the week, they can fit it into their workshop schedule and will
guarantee shipment in time. But I'm afraid the gown will have
to be completely paid for before I can place the order."

"*What?*" Mrs. Westwood put her hand to her throat as if

she was being assaulted. "Why on *earth* would ah have to pay for somethin' befowah ah've even laid *ahs* on it?"

"Yes, that seems a little odd to me, too," Charlotte added, her pretty little nose raised in the air.

Brianna took a slow, deep breath and kept smiling. "I'm afraid I can't order the gown any other way. This dress is being made up just for you, and cannot be returned. For *any* reason." At both of their indignant expressions, Brianna continued. "In the event that you find you don't want or can't use the gown, the likelihood that I would be able to sell the dress to another client is virtually nil. I'm sure you understand that I cannot absorb a twenty-thousand-dollar wedding dress into my inventory."

The two women gawked at her as if she had asked them to strip naked. Suddenly, Brianna had an almost overwhelming urge to laugh. Here in front of her sat Cinderella's mother and stepsister, their dual mission in life to intimidate anyone in their path. What did she care whether they did the wedding with her? If they didn't like how she ran her business, they could go elsewhere.

If they could find anyone else in town who would take them on.

A slow grin spread across her face as she leaned back in her chair, tapping her pen on the table in front of her. She felt like a poker player with a full house in hand. "So, ladies, that's the story. I'll be delighted to procure the dress for you, but once I fax the order to Paris, it's yours. For keeps."

The two brunettes—one natural, one not—exchanged a fleeting glance. Mrs. Westwood's jowls jiggled as she gave a half shake of her head at her daughter.

Sighing, Charlotte pursed her lips and said, "You know, I'm not sure whether I like that dress all that much anyhow. All that tulle…" She flapped her hand over her breasts. "I think it would make me look too busty, anyhow, don't you?" Then, with a bright smile that made Brianna inwardly cringe, Charlotte added, "Well, I guess that means starting over. Have you gotten in *anything* new since the last time I was in?"

"I'm sorry, Miss Westwood, but we only get new styles in twice a year, in December and June." A fact that she had told Charlotte at least three times. "So I'm afraid you've already seen everything we have. But I can always design something for you...."

Charlotte pouted and folded her arms across her chest. "Maybe I should go back to New York—"

Losing patience, Brianna cut her off. "If you remember, Miss Westwood, I just went to all the stores with Kelly less than a month ago. There's nothing there that I don't carry here. Nothing, anyway, important enough for the type of wedding you're having."

Another silent exchange passed between mother and daughter, then, "All right, Miss Fairchild, have it your way. I guess you'll have to make up something for me."

Brianna couldn't ever remember wanting to inflict physical injury on anyone, but right now she could have slapped Charlotte Westwood senseless and not had even a twinge of remorse. Had it not been for Spencer, she would have backed out of the contract, returned the Westwoods' money, and been done with it. But, in spite of the pain she felt whenever she thought of Spencer marrying this harpy, she wouldn't break her promise to handle his wedding for him.

"I'm sure we can come up with something that you'll be more than pleased with," Brianna said, pulling over a nearby sketchbook and flipping to a blank page. "I think something fitted, almost...*severe,* don't you?"

With a smirk, Brianna made a note to herself to talk to the seamstress about leaving a stray pin or two in the dress before Charlotte tried it on.

Having overseen probably two dozen or so weddings there, Brianna knew the staff well at the country club in Buckhead where Charlotte had decided to hold the reception, an institution where her family probably had had membership since Reconstruction. If not before. Brianna knew she was well liked—she never asked for anything impossible, and always gave more than enough notice for anything out-of-the ordinary that she might need. But when she called to confirm the largest banquet room for Charlotte's wedding, the manager went silent.

"What is it, Phil?"

He sighed. "Oh, nothing, really. Let's just say that, if we have to hold *this* wedding, at least *you're* the one in charge."

"Lord, that young woman really cuts a swath of destruction wherever she goes, doesn't she?"

"Like Sherman," came the dry reply on the other end of the line. "I suppose she would like the Atlanta Symphony to play a few dance tunes?"

"Actually, we haven't discussed music yet, but I'll keep that in mind," Brianna said with a laugh. "Think they might be free that evening?"

Her laugh was returned. "Just try to get across to her that my name's Phillip Johnston, not David Copperfield. I can't pull a thousand matching orchids out of my hat at the last minute."

"Not to worry. That's the florist's problem, anyway. Besides, I think she understands the words *final decision* now. You know me, Phil—I don't let 'em get away with anything."

"True enough, my dear. Well, the hall's yours, and you know we'll do what we can."

"Thanks, Phil. I'll be over...let's see..." She paged through her appointment book. "How's Tuesday at three sound?"

"See you then."

Brianna had no sooner hung up the phone when it rang with a piercing *brrrrr*. Her heart pounding, she pounced on it like a cat on a cricket.

"Fairchild's. May I help you?"

"Brianna?"

She took in a sharp breath. The voice was unmistakable, even twelve thousand miles away.

"Mr. Lockhart! What...what can I do for you?"

A robin trill outside her open window filled the second or

so before he responded. "I just thought I'd call to see how everything was going."

The receiver stuck to her sweaty palm. "Everything's just fine on this end."

"I take it…you're feeling better?"

She cringed at the concern in his voice. "Oh…yes…thank you."

"Was it the flu?"

"Uh…n-no. Probably just something I ate."

"Oh." A pause. "Have you been out to the house again since…since I left?"

Brianna nodded as if he could see her through the phone. "Yes, a couple of times. Your mother's very good at making sure I arrive at lunchtime so she can feed me. As it happens, I've got another appointment with her the day after tomorrow."

"Sounds as if she's adopted you."

"Yes, I think she has. Not that I mind."

"So you like the old girl?"

Were they having the conversation they seemed to be having? The words seemed innocuous enough, but both of them were having difficulty getting those words out. Brianna, for one, had a lump in her throat the size of Savannah. "I like her a great deal. In fact, she reminds me just a bit of my own mother."

The silence that followed was so long that she thought they'd lost their connection.

"Mr. Lockhart?"

When he finally responded, she could feel the caress in his voice from half a world away. "Be sure to ask Mother to show you the west garden. The tulips should be…outstanding about now."

"I—I'll be sure to do that." She felt tears well up, threatening to spill over her lashes. *What is this game you're playing, Spencer Lockhart? What do you want from me?*

"Have you talked to Kelly recently?"

Swallowing hard, she managed to say, "Only electronically.

We've E-mailed and faxed each other quite a bit, though."
Brianna smiled, even as a tear jumped overboard and dribbled
down her cheek. "By the way, I think you're really going to
like her dress."

"Oh?"

"Mmm-hmm. No lace."

His laugh was quiet, enfolding her like a favorite sweater.
"That's not surprising. If my sister could figure out a way to
wear *cowboy boots* to her wedding, she would."

"And who says she's not?" Would he see through her teasing, understand she was using it as a defense mechanism?

"Wh—?"

"Just kidding." She twirled the phone cord around her fingers, wanting to hang on to the conversation a little longer, in
spite of how much it hurt. "How's the weather there?" she
asked on an exhaled breath.

"Raining. Constantly. I should be selling them umbrellas."

"Oh…that's too bad. It's been glorious here. All the fruit
trees are in bloom."

There was a faint crackling on the line before she heard,
"It must be beautiful."

Then she laughed. Even to her ears, the sound was forced.
"Listen to me! As if they don't have fruit trees in Japan!"

His voice was so low she could hardly hear it. "I'd rather
be seeing them there." She heard a faint ringing on the other
end of the line. "Damn—I've got to get that. The hotel ran
another line into my room. Brianna—?"

"Yes?"

"Just…take care."

"You, too," she answered. But he had already hung up.

Brianna stared at the phone, her brows pulled together so
tightly her head hurt. Hot tears streamed down her cheeks
unchecked as she pushed her hands back through her hair and
shook her head slowly from side to side. *Why, why, why are
you doing this to me?* she screamed silently, burying her wet
face in her hands.

This was not going to work. Dabbing at her eyes with a

tissue, she wished there was some way she could get out of doing Charlotte's wedding at least, if not Kelly's as well. There was no way she could just ignore the agony she felt every time she came into contact with Spencer.

But backing out was not an option, and she knew it. Which meant she'd just have to muddle through as best she could. With a sigh, she picked up some orders that needed to be placed, but couldn't tell what she was looking at. It was at least five minutes before any of the papers on her desk made any sense.

And another several minutes before it struck her that not once during their entire conversation had Spencer mentioned his fiancée.

Spencer handled the call that had interrupted his conversation with Brianna as quickly as possible, then collapsed back in his chair with a groan. Her presence was so real to him, even that far away, that his fingers felt as if they had touched her. He could smell her sweet, floral scent in the cold, impersonal hotel room; if he closed his eyes, he could conjure up the image of her freckle-dusted face, that magic smile, those luminous green-gold eyes, her shimmering golden hair.

It was no good.

Still in his pajamas and robe, he got up and walked over to the picture window in his hotel room that overlooked Tokyo's skyline. It was only 7:00 a.m, but a thick haze of pollution had already swallowed up the tops of many of the skyscrapers. His brain had been in a similar haze most of the time he'd been in Japan.

Now, after that impulsive phone call, the haze had begun to lift.

He could not marry Charlotte.

As he crossed into the kitchenette to get a cup of coffee, he had the distinct feeling he was about to witness the redefinition of the adage, "Hell hath no fury like a woman scorned." Charlotte was not likely to take the news very gracefully.

But that was only part of his dilemma. Considering his actions to date, Brianna would probably want to have nothing to do with him. Although there was something in her voice when they spoke just now that gave him hope.

Hope. He never thought he'd live to see the day when he *hoped* to have a woman love him. But then, he never thought the day would come again when he'd be this much in love.

Completely enthralled, Brianna stood at the edge of the Lockharts' west garden, her hands nestled into the pockets of her white cotton cardigan. Tens of thousands of tulips, now blooming in broad rivers of scarlet and yellows and pinks and lavenders, spread out in front of her in a fairy-tale setting unlike anything she had ever seen. Spencer's mother stood beside her, managing to still look regal in a pair of periwinkle sweats, her expression bordering on the religious.

"Spencer's Daddy loved flowers," she said in a hushed voice, as if afraid her normal boom would disturb them. "Believe it or not, he planted most of these himself. Took *years* before he got them all in the ground." Edwina sighed. "Some of these bulbs are nearly forty years old, and still come up every year."

After a moment, Brianna asked, "You and Spencer's father had a good marriage, didn't you?"

"We thought so," she said with a grin. "Oh, we had an argument or two along the way—no two human beings are going to share thirty-five years of their lives and not disagree from time to time—but I never doubted that he loved me, not for one moment." With a wink for emphasis, she added, "And I never gave him any reason to doubt my love for him." Looking out over the extravagant display in her garden, she said, "I'm glad the flowers come up every year. Makes me think he's come to visit."

"Do you miss him very much?"

"It's been five years, so it doesn't hurt so much anymore. But I'll always miss him." She regarded Brianna with a pointedness that made her nervous. "But the feelings we shared were more than worth the missing now. I know what it feels like to be really, truly loved.''

Brianna blushed under the old woman's scrutiny and refocused her attention on the flowers. ''They're unbelievable.'' Then she laughed. ''I don't dare tell my poor little guys in my garden about this. Nothing will ever bloom again!''

''Ah…so you're a flower-lover, too?'' Edwina said, hooking her arm in the crook of Brianna's elbow as they started walking back to the house. A soft breeze teased Brianna's pastel-flowered challis skirt, the hem tickling her calves.

''What with the demands of the business, I don't have much time to coddle anything, so everything's pretty much on its own. But yes, I love gardening. I've got lots of bulbs, too—'' Brianna shook her head, grinning. ''Well, to me, it seems like a lot! Although, this year, I couldn't stand the smell of the narcissus when they came up. I had to cut them down before they were spent.''

After several seconds, she felt a slight squeeze on her elbow. Then, in a voice softer than Brianna could have imagined possible from the big woman, Edwina said, ''I couldn't stand the smell of narcissus when I was pregnant, either.''

Brianna froze and lowered her eyes, unable to move.

''So… I was right,'' Edwina said kindly.

Her knees as shaky as if she'd just gotten off a roller coaster ride, Brianna pulled out of Edwina's light grasp and made her way over to a nearby bench, managing to sit before her joints gave way. She didn't protest when Edwina sat beside her. ''How did you know?''

''Oh, come on, honey. It wasn't really that difficult to figure out. Especially since you seem to be going through the same symptoms I went through with both of mine. I knew that was no *flu* that made you so sick that morning a couple of weeks ago.'' She grinned and leaned toward her. ''And now that your appetite's back, you're eating like a horse. You've made quite a hit with the cook.''

In shock, Brianna sat speechless on the bench. Edwina put her hand on her forearm.

"I'm sorry. I suppose I should've kept my big mouth shut." The older woman sighed. "But you just seemed to need a *friend*. This is no time for a woman to be alone."

Brianna shook her head slowly, then choked back a sob. It clearly didn't matter one whit to this woman how she'd become pregnant. The tears welled up and spilled over, and she collapsed like a baby herself into Edwina's arms, letting the older woman's shushes and *there-there's* wash over her like a warm, soothing bath.

It was several minutes before Brianna's tears were spent. Finally she pulled herself upright and pulled a tissue out of her sweater pocket, blowing her nose.

"Do you want to talk about it?" Edwina asked.

Brianna spared her a brief, bleary-eyed glance, then gave a quick shake of her head.

"This child has a father, honey. Does he know?"

Brianna looked out over the garden, unseeing, worrying the crumpled-up tissue in her hand. "No."

"And...you're not going to tell him?"

A small laugh caught in Brianna's throat. "No. I don't think he'd be either delighted by or interested in the news." On a long, shaky sigh, she said, "Really, there's nothing to talk about. What's done is done, and I'm the only one who can deal with this." When she at last turned toward Edwina, a shaft of sunlight stung her tender eyes. "I just have one thing to ask of you."

"Name it," came the immediate reply.

Brianna took the older woman's large, knuckly hands in hers. "Please don't tell Spencer."

7

Spencer tore off the clothes he'd been wearing for fourteen straight hours in taxis and on planes and in airports and flung them across the bed, impatient with the buttons on the madras sport shirt he'd changed into. He slipped into a pair of chinos and loafers, then grabbed his keys off the hall table, not even bothering to check his answering machine for messages. They could wait. Everything could wait. Except this. Maybe this was foolish, he thought as he sprinted down the steps, but for once in his life he was going to act on his impulses, instead of weighing every damn option to death and coming up with nothing.

The early May evening was caressingly warm. He let the windows down in the car as he drove, enjoying the relatively clean air of Atlanta after the smog-ridden mess that hovered over Tokyo. He frowned, remembering his arrival a couple of hours earlier.

He hadn't expected Charlotte to meet him at the airport. It was everything he could do not to let his consternation show when he saw her bouncing up and down and waving at him at the gate. Then, in the limo on the way to her condo, she had been all over him, more amorous than she had been the entire previous year they had been dating.

Too little, too late. There was nothing Charlotte Westwood could do now that would even remotely arouse him.

Her expression was priceless when he turned down her unspoken offer of preconjugal bliss. The fact that she had accepted his suggestion that they refrain from being intimate until after the wedding was nothing short of amazing. Why couldn't he have taken it one step further? He knew he had no intention of marrying Charlotte, so why didn't he just tell her, right then, in the car, and be done with it?

Why, indeed?

Instead, he'd copped out, feeling like a louse when he dropped her off, leaving her to think that everything was normal—except, perhaps, for a libido on hiatus—when all he was really thinking of was what he was about to say to the woman he loved so much it scared him.

And now he pulled up in front of Brianna's house, wondering just exactly how he was going to go about this. He forked his hand through his hair and let out an enormous sigh.

She couldn't put it off any longer. The groceries were not going to buy themselves, and the way she was eating these days, she didn't dare let things get to the peanut-butter-and-jar-of-olives stage like she used to when she was a student. Her favorite white eyelet sundress strangling her midsection, Brianna skipped down the back stairs, her feet barely making a sound in her rope-soled shoes. Remembering she'd parked out front, she crossed through the waiting room, backing out of the front door and locking it.

"Brianna?"

Her hand flew to her chest as she whirled around to see Spencer leaning against the newel post at the bottom of her porch steps.

"What on earth are you doing here?" she snapped, breathing hard. She immediately softened at the look of stunned disappointment on his face. "I'm sorry. You just startled me. I don't surprise well, I'm afraid."

"You don't?" he asked, walking up the steps, closing in on her. Smiling.

She unconsciously stepped back as he came nearer, shaking her head and rattling to cover for the panic that was threatening to turn her knees into jelly. "Uh-uh. My parents tried to give me a surprise birthday party when I was six, and I was in hysterics for nearly an hour.'' She felt a weak smile pull at her lips. ''They never tried that again.''

''Brianna—''

She realized she could hardly breathe from trying so hard not to cry. She abruptly looked away, clasping her car keys in her left hand. ''I'm on my way to the grocery store.''

''How about having dinner with me instead?''

She forced herself to meet his eyes. ''Why in heaven's name would I do that?''

''Why not?''

Her mouth fell open. ''You must be dealing with serious jet lag.'' She pushed past him and stomped down the stairs. ''I don't make it a practice to go out to dinner with men who are engaged to someone else.''

She heard him take the steps two at a time behind her, felt his hand seize her arm. ''And I wouldn't ask you if I were.''

She whipped her head around to him, ignoring what his touch on her arm was doing to her heart rate. ''What are you talking about?''

''You were right. Everyone was right. I don't love Charlotte and I have no business marrying her.''

Brianna pulled away with a little jerk and cocked her head. ''You broke off the engagement?''

''I intend to, yes.''

''You *intend* to?'' Their gazes collided as she felt her blood pressure go through the roof. ''What kind of a fool do you think I am? I do have *some* pride, if you don't mind. Do you really think you can just show up, announce your intention to dispense with your fiancée, ask me to dinner, and go on from there—''

''Brianna, let me explain—''

''Forget it, Spencer.''

''For God's sake, I don't love Charlotte!''

''You never have! But you persisted in going through with this engagement anyway.'' Her skin was flushed; her head was beginning to pound from exasperation. ''This may come as a shock to you, but don't you think your actions the past few weeks may have skewed your credibility just the tiniest bit?'' She glared at him, watching his expression alter like quicksilver.

Then it dawned on her that whether or not he was engaged had nothing to do with their situation. There could be no relationship between them. Ever. So she said the first thing that popped into her head.

''Besides, did it ever occur to you that maybe I wasn't available?''

Every muscle in his face tensed. ''No,'' he said softly. ''It didn't.'' He looked away, just for a second, then turned back to her, his eyes dulled. ''There's someone else?''

With one hand, she fumbled for the newel post beside her. ''In a manner of speaking, yes.''

''You met someone while I was away?''

She shook her head. ''It happened before.''

''Before New York?''

She lowered her eyes, aware that her throat had suddenly become so dry she could hardly speak. ''I...didn't realize it was serious until...afterward.''

He clasped her shoulders, his grip surprisingly gentle considering the sparks in his eyes. ''Tell me you're in love with someone else,'' he said in a strained voice, ''and I'll never bother you again.''

That far, she couldn't go. Twisting the truth was one thing; lying was something else. Instead, she just shook her head and repeated, ''I'm simply not available, Spencer.''

He let go of her shoulders, throwing her just slightly off balance, and swiftly walked back to his car. There was no ''goodbye.'' Nothing. Just the sound of a car door slamming and tires crunching on gravel as he pulled out of her driveway and drove away.

Tonight. He would tell Charlotte tonight.

Spencer settled in for the drive to his fiancée's condo, the Tchaikovsky symphony on the radio making him more melancholy than he already was. No matter that the woman he had finally realized he loved had turned him down flat the day before. He still needed to sever his relationship with Charlotte.

They had dinner reservations with his mother and Kelly, who had just flown in that afternoon from New York. Afterward he would take her back to her condo, then tell her. He still had no idea in hell what he was going to say, but he figured the words would be there when the time came.

He hoped to God he'd be more successful with Charlotte than he had been with Brianna.

Charlotte opened her front door before he rang the bell. She was wearing purple again, a color he realized he detested.

"Good," she said, lifting her lips for a kiss, which he gave as quickly and noncommittally as he could. "You're early. Let's go."

"Our reservations aren't until six—"

"Kelly's having her fitting, you said?"

He frowned. "Yes…"

"Then we can meet your mother and sister at Fairchild's."

"There's no need. They'll meet us at the restaurant."

Charlotte picked her purse and a black challis shawl imprinted with a bright paisley design up from the hall table. "Miss Fairchild told me I could drop by and see if she's gotten around to making the mockup of my dress yet."

"Are you sure? I thought she only worked by appointment—"

With a snort of laughter, Charlotte swirled the shawl around her shoulders, shaking her head as if he just didn't understand the ways of women and weddings. "She'll make an exception for me, darlin'. You know," she added as she passed through her door, "If I didn't sit on that woman, she'd never get *anything* done. I really don't know why you hired her in the first place."

There was no point in commenting. In a few hours, Charlotte's views on Brianna's professionalism would be moot. For the moment, however, it seemed wisest to just let Charlotte think she was running the show.

* * *

"*Now* I'm getting excited."

"Well, you should. It's only three weeks until the wedding," Brianna said, fidgeting with one of the sleeves on Kelly's dress.

Kelly studied herself as if she wasn't quite sure she was seeing her own reflection, then grinned in the three-way mirror at Brianna, standing behind her. "You know, if more dresses looked like this, I'd be much more inclined to wear them."

Brianna smiled. "Mmm...but can you imagine wearing something like this in the subway? I don't think so."

"What subway? Only a gilded coach would do with this gown." She tilted her head and sighed. "This is one gorgeous dress, that's for sure."

It was. The gossamer tissue taffeta, the color of the palest pink peony, was perfect with Kelly's nearly translucent skin. Dozens of tiny pin tucks skimmed the bride's tall, slender figure from the wide, nearly off-the-shoulder neckline to the top of her hips, where a profusion of overlapping taffeta and organza petals that formed the skirt floated around Kelly's slender legs and ankles. Echoing the skirt, tapered layers of organza formed the merest suggestion of sleeves, the point of each layer weighted by a single, tiny, tear-shaped pearl.

The jury was still out on whether or not she should wear a veil, but, after much deliberation, it had been decided that Kelly would pull her white-blond hair back from her face into a chignon around which she would wear a circlet of white and pale pink miniature roses and baby's breath. On the day itself the flowers would be real, but for now the milliner had crafted a substitute for the suggested headpiece from some silk flowers she had in stock. Brianna pinned the circlet around the bun that Kelly had hurriedly pinned up, then pivoted Kelly around so her mother could see her.

"So...what do you think?"

Edwina Lockhart, the most dressed up Brianna had ever seen her in her vintage Chanel suit and bow-tied silk blouse, sat in one of the worn armchairs with her long legs crossed, her chin sunk into her hand. Her pale blue eyes were sheened with I-refuse-to-cry tears.

"Who'd've thought I'd get the chance to see what my baby'd look like if she were an angel?" Her voice was remarkably soft, for her. Then the spark returned to the eyes and the voice once again plummeted as she added, "Which we *all* know she isn't."

"Oh, Momma!"

"Oh, Momma!" Edwina mimicked her daughter with a broad smile, then made a shooing motion with her large hands. "Now, you go on and get out of that dress and hightail your little behind out of here. I've got some things to discuss with Brianna."

After Kelly had been duly reattired in her customary jeans and man-tailored shirt and led off by Zoe, Brianna turned to Edwina with an arched eyebrow. "What did I do now?"

"I'm not sure." She patted the empty chair next to hers. "I'm just being a mother, that's all. Sit for a second. I want to know how you're doing."

Obediently, Brianna sat. "I'm doing just fine, Edwina."

"In spite of my son's making an idiot of himself?"

Brianna gave a little start. "He told you."

"Yes." Edwina squinted at her. "How're you handling this?"

"I told him—"

"Yes, I know what you told him. And I don't blame you one bit. That was a damn fool thing he did, ambushing you the way he did. But still…" She paused. "You know he's in love with you."

Funny—she hadn't heard that pronouncement from Spencer's lips. Brianna rose from her chair and started to hang up Kelly's gown, trying to keep her voice steady. "Why are you telling me this? I'm not exactly in a position to—"

"To return his affection? Or to tell him about the baby?"

She bit her lip. "Could we please change the subject?"

The old chair creaked as Edwina got up and moved over to Brianna. "All right." She paused, then rubbed the spot on

Brianna's back between her shoulder blades. "All you sure you're okay? You seem tired to me."

"Well, I *am* tired. I'm…"

"Yes, we know."

Brianna lifted her hands in a little helpless gesture, hoping she could keep the tears at bay. She was beginning to feel as if all she did these days was cry. "This may sound like the stupid remark of the century, but it's so *hard* doing this alone. And the baby's not even here yet."

Her deep gray brows knotted with concern, Edwina took Brianna by the shoulders and looked straight into her eyes. "Honey, it's hard doing this with *two* people. I can't imagine what you must be going through."

No wonder Spencer is so kind, Brianna thought as she stood in front of the man's mother, who wore compassion the way most women wore shoes. Except that Edwina Lockhart's concern came from deep within, from a never-depleted well of love and genuine sympathy for the trials of others. Brianna's mother had been like that. All it took was one look, one, "What's wrong, sweetie?" and Brianna would dissolve into tears.

With a rueful smile, Brianna considered how ironic it was that the one person who seemed ready and willing to listen to her troubles just happened to be the mother of one of those troubles.

Kelly poked her head in the doorway. "Spence and Charlotte are here."

Spencer! *And Charlotte?* Brianna's stomach yanked in sixteen different directions.

Edwina dropped her hands from Brianna's shoulders and shot a disapproving glance at her daughter. "They were supposed to meet us at the restaurant."

Kelly quickly surveyed the hallway, then stepped all the way inside the dressing room. "Charlotte wants to know if Brianna has the mockup yet for her dress," she said in a low voice, her eyes full of apology. "Sorry. There was no stopping her."

But you said the wedding was off, Spencer...

Her emotions still turning somersaults, Brianna discharged Kelly's concern with a forced little laugh. "And there's no pushing me, a fact which she has not yet come to terms with, apparently." She sighed. "I guess I'd better go out to her before..." A resigned shrug ended the sentence.

Both ladies both groaned in sympathy. But before Brianna could leave, Kelly caught her gently by the arm. "Listen—why don't you have dinner with us tonight?"

"Oh! No, I don't think—"

"Oh, come on, honey," Edwina encouraged. "It'll do you good."

Brianna stared at Edwina, panic rising in her throat like bursting lava. *What are you doing?* her eyes demanded, even as her mouth said, "But you already have reservations..."

"Oh, pooh..." Kelly said. "As many times as we've eaten at that place, there won't be any problem having an extra chair brought to the table."

"Now, I won't take no for an answer, young lady," Edwina said, squaring her shoulders.

As Brianna searched Edwina's face, sure that the woman had taken total leave of her senses for not only allowing, but *insisting* that she and her son be seated at the same dinner table, she heard Kelly whisper, "If I were you, I wouldn't even *think* about arguing."

Her fists clenched when she saw him. *Them.*

What was all that about? she wanted to scream at him. *If you were so hot to break off with her, why are you standing here with her, touching her, still clearly engaged to her?*

"Miss Fairchild," he said with a slight nod, his voice silkily low. The steel gray of his summer-weight suit and crisp white dress shirt set off his tanned-looking complexion, those intense blue eyes. Brianna had never been one to judge a man by his looks, but suddenly, in spite of her wishing she could just make the man disappear from her life forever, his sheer handsomeness just about knocked her six ways to Sunday.

"Kelly is just thrilled with what you're doing." He ensnared her eyes in his, searching her face for heaven-knew-what, even as his arm lightly rested against the royal purple fabric of his fiancée's dress. Or, was it that Charlotte leaned against *him?*

"Yes..." A wave of something unrecognizable nearly drowned her. Was it coming from him or her? She tried not to stammer. "Yes, the dress has turned out very well."

"So I've heard," he said with a smile.

With the sizzling suddenness of a lightning strike, she wanted him. All of him. In spite of the fact that he was clearly still engaged to Charlotte. In spite of the fact that she was pregnant and not in the market for a relationship with anyone. In spite of the fact that just thinking about Spencer infuriated her like a wasp whose nest has been attacked. She caught her breath at the realization. Had somebody traded places with her body when she wasn't looking? Brianna Fairchild just did not have feelings like this.

Ever.

It must be the hormones. Yes, that's it. She'd read in more than one book that pregnancy hormones can make women very...amorous, especially during the second trimester, which she was just starting. That had to be the only explanation for the unbidden, inexplicable surge of pure physical desire for Spencer that now shot through her with such intensity she could hardly breathe, multiplying tenfold every second longer he held her gaze in his. Heat emanated from her skin as if she'd been wired—she was positive her desire was palpable to everyone in the room.

And yet, the rage and hurt remained, undiminished by these new, frightening sensations. She almost winced as the sweet memory of the feel of his lips on hers flooded her senses as clearly as if they were locked in an embrace right now. Then she noticed that Spencer was not breathing normally, either, although he was exerting great effort not to let it show. His smile barely masked his pain; his eyes told her he felt exactly the way she did.

And he could not blame *his* state on pregnancy.

Brianna tore her eyes from his, feeling at that moment that her current mental state was far more scandalous than the act that brought about the baby growing in her womb.

She forced herself to turn to Charlotte. "Miss Westwood," she said in a flat voice, willing the flush in her cheeks to subside. "Kelly said you had a question?"

"Just wondering if the mockup of my dress is ready?"

Brianna managed a smile. "I'm afraid not. Next Tuesday, isn't that what we had agreed on?"

A hint of a frown fluttered across Charlotte's too perfectly plucked eyebrows. "Yes, my appointment was for Tuesday, I just thought…"

"And I promise we'll be ready then. Will your mother be joining us?"

She didn't catch Charlotte's reply. What she *did* catch was Spencer's glare at his fiancée and the woman's subsequent nervous smile at him in return.

Brianna had insisted on taking her own car to the riverfront restaurant so no one would have to take her home afterward; if nothing else, the solitary drive had given her some time to give her hormones a good talking-to, so that she could at least appear to be in control when she had to face Spencer again.

That had been the plan.

However, within five minutes of their arrival, Brianna realized she should have put her foot down with Mrs. Lockhart and simply refused to join them. She could have pleaded illness, previous plans, anything. Submitting to this evening was clearly going to be an exercise in masochism.

She wondered how much Edwina had told her daughter, how much both of them could pick up from the charged air. Seated between the two Lockhart ladies in such a way that her peripheral vision still caught their expressions, Brianna sensed the shared raised eyebrows, and then, much worse, the mother-daughter conspiratorial smile. It seemed, however, that Charlotte was so wrapped up in herself and her Manhattans that she didn't notice anything right away. Brianna took advantage of the situation as long as she could.

"Are you headed back to New York after the weekend?" she asked Kelly.

Kelly shook her head as she munched on a piece of roll. "I'm back here until the wedding. I got my coursework all finished early so I can stick around."

"Poor Colin!" Brianna smiled. "How's he faring all alone?"

"Not well, judging from his last phone call," Kelly said with a grin. "In fact, I think he's going to find a sub for his classes for the rest of the term and join me down here."

"That doesn't sound very politic to me," Spencer interjected.

Kelly waved her hand at him. "It's okay, really. Even the profs take off from time to time." She wiped her mouth on her napkin and took a sip of wine, then added, "Besides, I need him here."

Spencer sounded unconvinced. "It just seems to me he's sidestepping his responsibility."

"Oh, Spence," his mother cut in, "don't be such a hardnose. Colin's one of the most conscientious young men I've ever met."

"That's right." Kelly gave an enthusiastic nod of her head, her pale hair glinting in the subtle overhead spotlights. "All his lesson plans are done for the rest of the semester. Anyone could take over."

Although the two Lockhart women did not seem unduly upset by Spencer's objections to his future brother-in-law's actions, Brianna could see his jaw tighten. Why she felt the need to diffuse his concern, she didn't know. But before she fully realized the words had slipped out of her mouth, she said, "Colin certainly seemed to be a very together young man when I met him. Everyone has their own way of dealing with their responsibilities, Mr. Lockhart. I'm sure no harm will come to anyone if he chooses to spend the few weeks before his wedding with his fiancée."

It was a simple gesture. Hardly anything, really. Spencer just raised his wineglass to her and, with what could barely be considered a smile, said, "You're absolutely correct, Miss Fairchild."

His gaze, piercing through the half light allowed by the cluster of candles on the table, sent her blood racing again.

And Charlotte saw it.

Her reaction was not obvious at first, except maybe to Brianna, who did not miss the slight narrowing of the dark eyes, the full mouth pulling itself into a straight line. As dinner was served—along with Charlotte's third Manhattan—it would have seemed to an uninvolved listener that the conversation among the five people at their table was normal, cordial, unremarkable.

But by the time they were halfway through the main course, Charlotte had turned from a well-mannered, extremely refined—if a little flamboyant—young woman, into an insecure shrew. At first, she paid no heed whatsoever to Brianna, preferring to overcompensate by monopolizing the attention of her unamused fiancé. She hardly took her hands, let alone her eyes, off of Spencer the rest of the evening, nearly curdling Brianna's stomach with the constant, cloying terms of endearment oozing from her painstakingly painted lips.

"Spencer, darlin', would you *please* pass the salt?" she'd wheeze, when it was nearly as close to her as it was to him.

Or, "Spencer, honey, I'd just *love* some more rolls, wouldn't you? Please have the waiter bring some over."

Then, "Spencer, sugar, would you please check my face? I'll just *die* of embarrassment if I have any food on it." Brianna had squirmed, remembering New York and hot dogs and Spencer's burning touch on her own face, as Charlotte tilted her pretty face up to her fiancé's with a coquettish bat of the eyes and pouting red lips.

Brianna's usual propensity these days for devouring everything in sight vanished, and the succulent honey-cured ham in front of her remained pretty much untouched. She wondered if anyone noticed that she'd spent the better part of the past half hour pushing the same few green beans from one part of her plate to another and back again.

Then the attacks started.

At first, Charlotte's gibes were little more than pathetic, juvenile attempts to gain the upper hand. But in Brianna's addled emotional state, they still hit their marks more often than not.

"You know, Miss Fairchild, I've been meaning to speak to you about the state of the salon?"

Brianna felt the hair bristle on the back of her neck. Turning a statement into a question, which Brianna noticed that Charlotte did quite often, put Brianna instantly on alert. "Oh?"

"Yes... I noticed the other day that the wallpaper is really getting pretty shabby in places, don't you think?"

Brianna nodded, watching in amazement as Charlotte actually buttered her own roll. "I couldn't agree more. In fact, I hope to have the salon redone in the fall."

"The *fall?*" Charlotte uttered the word as if meant something vile. "Now, honey, you and I both know that those drapes are *not* going to make it that long. Why, you could practically *plant* things in the folds, they're so dusty."

Brianna stiffened. She knew the furnishings in the salon were a little long in the tooth, but they were not dirty. The carpet, upholstery, and drapes were cleaned every six months. But to mention that fact would just add fuel to the fire—she knew Charlotte was looking for an argument.

"Is that so?" Brianna replied quietly. "I guess I'd been so busy I'd hadn't noticed. I'll be sure to have it taken care of, Miss Westwood."

She could feel Spencer's eyes on her, feel his increasing irritation with his fiancée. But he dared not speak on her behalf, or the beast would become fully unleashed. Like Brianna, he would not want a scene in a public place.

However, his mother had no such compunction.

"As long as Miss Fairchild is taking good care of you, I don't think you need concern yourself about a little dust on the curtains, Charlotte.'' The older woman's voice was menacingly level.

Charlotte's eyes narrowed. "And who says she's taking good care of me?"

"Charlotte..." Spencer's voice was like iron.

"Well, it's true, Spencer," she whined, pouting like a toddler. "I wanted that dress from Paris, and she *refused* to get it for me."

Brianna sighed. "I did not refuse to order the gown...."

Charlotte nodded, the slash of red mouth menacing in the flickering candlelight on the table. "No, that's right, Miss Fairchild. But you as good as *blackmailed* me into backing off. Said there was no returning the dress once it was here, that it was mine *whether I used it or not*." She paused, to gain the fullest effect, then said, "I just wondered what you meant by that."

"I didn't mean anything except that I couldn't accept the dress back into stock," Brianna replied, wearily rubbing the space between her eyes.

"Well, *I* think you meant something *very* specific. You don't think I'm going to marry Spencer, do you? You don't *want* me to marry Spencer." She staggered to her feet, whipping her arm out of Spencer's grasp as he tried to make her sit down. "You don't want me to marry Spencer so you can have him to yourself...."

"Charlotte!" Fury bled through his tenuous control. "That will do. Now *sit down*."

Ignoring her fiancé, Charlotte leaned over the table, her face eerily underlit from the candles.

"So you'll have a father for your *baby!*"

"*Charlotte!* What the *hell* are you talking about?"

Brianna sat immobile, grateful for the press of Mrs. Lockhart's hand underneath the table, feeling the heat from Charlotte's triumphant leer.

"Momma noticed it right off. Said that she can always tell when someone's got one in the oven. And I've never known her to be wrong...."

"Well, she's wrong this time, Charlotte—"

"No, Spencer, she's not." Brianna picked her napkin off her lap and loosely folded it, then lay it by her plate. Her movements were slow and deliberate, as if she were in a dream. Now she met his stunned eyes without even a trace of guilt or remorse or discretion, no longer afraid of what she would find. "It's true. I'm going to have a baby in October." *I'm sorry. So very, very sorry,* she let her eyes say for her. "Now, if you don't mind…" She turned to Spencer's mother. "I think that was my cue to leave."

As she stood, Edwina grabbed her hand. "I don't think you should attempt driving home alone…"

Brianna squeezed her hand, shaking her head. "Believe it or not, I'm fine. In fact, I feel better about things than I've felt in a couple of months."

Brianna's calm acquiescence to Charlotte's accusation must have had nearly the same effect as several cups of strong coffee on Charlotte's bloodstream. By the time she got in Spencer's car, she was stone-cold sober, if not entirely contrite. And, judging from the frightened-deer look in her eyes, she was scared silly of what Spencer might say to her.

With good reason.

With the possible exception of his mother, his sister, and his remarkably efficient secretary, Spencer would have been more than happy that night to consign the rest of the female sex to a remote space station. He wasn't sure whether he was more upset with Charlotte or Brianna for that disastrous evening, but as his fiancée currently occupied the glove-leather bucket seat next to his, she was the one who first received the brunt of his anger.

He didn't dare speak at all for several minutes as he drove her home, his hand gripping the steering wheel so hard he could feel the imprint of the textured leather rim imbedded in the palm of his hand. If the truth be known, he wasn't sure *what* he felt about Brianna's situation. He was far too shocked to think clearly about that. But he had no doubt whatsoever about Charlotte. He could have understood prewedding nerves, even jealousy. Vindictiveness, however, was another story.

Charlotte stared straight ahead at the road, motionless except for her constant worrying of her engagement ring with the fingers of her right hand. Finally, she spoke, her voice strained and apprehensive.

"I'm sorry, Spence—"

He raised his right hand, cutting her off. "Don't waste your breath, Charlotte. It's over. The engagement's off."

Damn. He could have slapped himself for blurting it out like that. But there it was.

"*No!* Oh, Spencer, please, *please,* give me another chance..."

"Why should I?" He ground out the words. "Your behavior tonight was unconscionable." His eyes flicked in her direction, then back out to the road. "Do you have the slightest idea how your ridiculous display might have made anyone else feel? But then, you must have. I've never seen anyone so deliberately set out to hurt someone else the way you did that poor woman."

He thought he might have heard her sniffle in the silence. Then, "It's true, isn't it? You do love her?"

He considered, then decided he didn't want to tell her.

"Let's put it this way. I think a hell of a lot more of Miss Fairchild at this moment, pregnant or not, than I think of you."

"I see." She studied the darkness out her window. "Is the baby yours?"

A sharp laugh flew from his throat. "I can't believe you're even *asking* me this question."

"Well, excuse me," she snapped, whipping her head back around. "But I just spent an evening wondering if I was about to be singed from the heat between you two, and she's pregnant... It hardly seems an illogical question, now does it?"

When he didn't immediately answer her, Charlotte leaned against her window, gnawing on a cuticle, tiny whimpering sounds filling the space between them. Finally, Spencer said with a quiet sigh, "No, Charlotte, the baby's not mine. I am

not having, nor have I had, an affair with Brianna Fairchild."
Spencer exhaled loudly and shifted his right hand to the steering wheel, propping his left elbow up on doorside armrest and leaning his head in his hand. "God knows I've tried to make it work with you, Charlotte. I really have. But I think we're beating a dead horse here, and you know it."

After a long pause, she said, "This has nothing to do with tonight at all, does it?"

He had no choice but to be honest. "Not really."

"You've never loved me."

He glanced at her profile in the alternating darkness and flashes of light as they passed under the highway lights. "This is no surprise, surely?"

She gave a deep, shaky sigh. "No, it isn't." He heard her dress rustle as she shifted to face him. "But you know I love *you.* And I thought you at least *liked* me. I guess I had always hoped that eventually you'd come around."

"Oh, Charlotte—I *do* care about you. I wouldn't have let things get this far if I didn't. And I swear I would have been a faithful husband to you, so help me God."

"Would have?" The words were spoken quietly, more to herself, as if trying to grasp their reality. As she shook her head, he heard her curls whisper against the silk of her dress, then sensed her pleading eyes watching him. *"Please* don't break up with me, Spence. I'll do anything you want. I'll even apologize to Miss Fairchild."

They had reached Charlotte's condo. Spencer pulled up in front, cut the engine, and closed his eyes, desperately trying to sort out his thoughts, to regain the control he had given up the night before with Brianna.

It wasn't that simple.

He remembered the decision he had made in Japan, after weeks of agonizing deliberation; the shock he had felt when Brianna admitted the truth of Charlotte's allegation; the outrage that still burned through him at his fiancée's heinous behavior.

But most of all, he remembered Brianna's beautiful, honest

face, and the way their one kiss had made him feel as though he had found something he hadn't even known was missing.

He no longer knew whether his heart or his head was making the decisions.

He no longer cared.

He got out of the car and went around to Charlotte's door. After opening it and assisting her out as he had always done, he held her by the shoulders, less than a foot from his face. Judging from the smile that began creeping across her lips, she apparently thought he was about to kiss her. About to make up.

"It really doesn't matter what you decide to do," he said, his mouth taut. "It won't change my mind."

Then he watched as the pleading expression in her eyes grew flint-like, like an animal cornered, ready to defend its territory. "Oh, no?" she said, the edges of her teeth glinting from between her half-smiling lips in the darkness. "Don't count on it."

She pulled away from his grasp and slowly ascended the steps to her condo, her ample derriere oscillating in front of him like an enchanted cobra.

8

A pair of bickering squirrels embroiled in a hot-and-heavy territorial dispute just outside Brianna's bedroom window woke her up at some ungodly hour the following Monday morning. Her brain still fogged with sleep, she rolled over onto her side and observed the antics of the little gray beasts in the old oak, until the brouhaha was settled in a flash of twitching tails and ear-piercing chatter. Afterward, the victor leveled bright eyes at her from his perch not four feet away as if to say, "So what are you staring at?" then scampered out of sight, leaving a rustle of leaves in his wake.

Brianna nestled back on her pillow, her hand automatically spreading across her abdomen. She knew it was too early to feel anything yet, but she checked every morning, just the same. She hoped, with a desperateness she could barely admit even to herself, that feeling her child's quickening might alleviate her almost constant heavy-heartedness.

The weekend weddings had kept her sufficiently busy so that she had not had time or energy to think about Friday night's fiasco, or Spencer, or how she felt about any of it. And, as she lay in bed listening to the excited twitters of finches and robins heralding the new spring day, she made a conscious decision to keep the whole tangled mess on her brain's back burner for one more day at least.

Yawning, she enjoyed a luxurious stretch in the flood of sunshine washing over the bed, and felt the call of damp soil and spades and little green sprouts shooting up from the earth.

It was a day for gardening, she decided, not ruminating about things she could not change.

After a breakfast that would have put a hard hat to shame, Brianna threw on a white T-shirt and an old chambray jumper that fell from her shoulders to the middle of her calves in a simple A-line, its only adornment being two enormous pockets over her thighs. She caught a glimpse of herself in the cheval mirror in the corner of her bedroom and stood sideways, pulling out the front of the oversize garment, sucking in her breath at the realization of what she was going to look like in a few months.

Unbelievable.

Shaking her head, she grabbed her purse and keys and headed out the door.

An hour later, her van harboring a good portion of the bedding plant inventory of a nearby nursery, she turned back onto her street, her stomach knotting when she noticed Spencer's Towncar parked in her driveway.

Oh, no. Not today.

He was leaning against the side of his car with his arms folded against his chest. Ready for a round of golf, maybe, she thought as she pulled up into the drive, not spending the day behind a desk.

"I was afraid I'd missed you," he said, coming around to the driver's side and opening her door for her. His face was drawn, as if he hadn't slept well.

What was she supposed to do now? Stalling until she could think of something to say, she released the hatch and got out of the van, trying not to brush against him as she went around to the back. She flung up the hatch, then reached into the car to retrieve a flat of multicolored impatiens.

"Brianna?" His low, soft voice caressed her as surely as if he'd touched her.

She turned awkwardly with the flat wobbling in her hands. He had been standing right behind her; she nearly rammed the flat into his stomach. "Why do you keep doing this?"

He took the tray from her, his brows furrowed. "Doing what?"

"Showing up on my doorstep. Making me crazy." She took out another flat, this one filled with snapdragons and spicy, fragrant stock.

He lay the flat he had taken from her on the low wall next to the driveway, then caught her by the shoulders. "We need to talk."

She flinched at the touch of his warm hands through her cotton T-shirt as she looked up at him, squinting in the sun. "I don't see that there's much point in that," she said, shrugging off his grasp. She carried the plants over to the shady porch and set them down on the steps.

"Yes, there is," he said as he followed her. "Charlotte was way out of line Friday night. I would have called you, but I knew you were tied up all weekend. Besides, I wanted to say this in person."

Brianna passed him on the way back to the car. "To say what?" she asked over her shoulder. She picked up the last tray, full of glowing cerise, purple, and white petunias, then crossed back to the porch. "I don't expect you to apologize for Charlotte," she said, slightly out of breath. "Besides, it's no big deal."

His hand landed on her upper arm, halting her flight. "I don't believe that."

With a sigh, she pulled away from him again and set the flat on the porch next to the others. "Look, I've had better nights in my life, I grant you, but she didn't say anything that isn't going to be public knowledge in a few weeks anyway." Pushing her hair off her face with her wrist, she gave a quick shake of her head. "Neither you, nor Charlotte, owe me anything. Least of all an apology. Just forget it."

She walked to the back of the car and slammed down the hatch, noticing out of the corner of her eye that Spencer had seated himself on her porch steps, his hands knotted together between his knees. What was he waiting for? The lemonade to be served?

"I told Charlotte it was over," he said.

"Oh, did you now?" she parried, unable to keep the sarcasm out of her voice.

"I said I was going to, didn't I?"

After a moment of wrestling with herself, Brianna slowly approached him, one hand shielding her eyes from the sun. The closer she got, the broader Spencer's smile became, the little creases in his face softened in the dappled light on the porch steps. She shook her head as she wiped dirt from her hands, feeling as if she'd just gotten off a carnival ride.

"For your sake, I'm glad it's over," she said quietly, over the feeling of light-headedness. "But it doesn't change anything." She saw the smile dim, just a little, as she leaned one hand against the porch railing, tucking the other one into her pocket. "I told you that nothing could happen between us."

"And now I know why you said that," he said gently. "That's the 'other person' you were talking about, isn't it? The baby?"

She met his gaze briefly, then nodded just once. Then, before he could speak again, she said, "It does make a difference, doesn't it?"

Spencer focused on his hands for a long time before replying. "I've thought of nothing else all weekend, just trying to figure out *what* I thought." He looked up at her, his eyes almost the same shade of ultramarine as his knit shirt. "I'll admit, I was shocked Friday night. And I don't shock easily."

Brianna folded her arms across her ribs and leaned her side against the post. "I don't imagine you do."

After a long moment, he patted the space next to him on the step. "Sit. Please."

Not unwillingly, she complied, lacing her fingers over her knees as she focused on the pulsating tessellation of sun and shade dancing across her front lawn.

"Are you listening?"

She nodded.

"I had already realized that marrying Charlotte would be disastrous, especially for her in the long run. But when I told you I was going to break up with her, I hadn't yet realized how difficult that was going to be.'' He smiled wryly. "I don't have much experience with breaking engagements. And I'd rather face a group of angry Teamsters than thwart Charlotte... Oh, good—you can still smile.''

She turned to him, her head resting in her hand. "Sometimes.''

He reached up and grazed her jaw with one finger. "That smile is why I'm sitting here right now. Why I realized that how I felt about you couldn't change, no matter what surprises you may have in store for me.''

When she abruptly looked away, she felt his hand come to rest, lightly, on her back.

"Look, can we...is it all right if we go inside?'' he asked. "We don't need every nosy resident of Inwood Park watching us.''

With a short nod, she got up and took him around to the back of the house, where they went through the old-fashioned screen door and up the creaking narrow staircase that led directly to her apartment. It seemed entirely logical that she should bring him here, and yet, as she stood in the middle of her living room with her hands squashed down into the pockets of her jumper, she found herself at a loss for rational thoughts, let alone words.

"Would you like some iced tea?'' she said at last.

"Only if it's already made,'' he replied with a shrug and a smile that almost brought the tears all by itself.

She nodded, deciding that if he didn't touch her, she just might get through this.

Without thinking, he followed her into the kitchen, leaning one hip on the counter and watching her as she pulled two glasses down from the cabinet. When he noticed her shaking hands, however, he took the hint and turned his attention elsewhere.

He walked over to the door between the kitchen and the living room, scanning the spacious room with an appreciative eye. Her tastes were clearly eclectic, Mission next to Colonial in front of Chippendale alongside French Provincial, all effortlessly pulled together on top of an enormous Persian rug in the colors of a Middle Eastern bazaar. A puff of breeze stirred, then billowed out three sets of sheer white draperies hung almost haphazardly across black iron rods over open floor-to-ceiling windows, as triple shafts of midmorning sun exposed thousands of dust motes suspended like fairy dust in air fragranced with honeysuckle, roses, petunias, jasmine.

"Your apartment is beautiful. Pretty much just the way I'd imagined it."

She handed him his tea with a nervous smile. "Really?"

"Mmm-hmm. The warm colors, the light streaming in, even the fragrance. It's you." He took a sip of the tea and nodded toward the china cabinet on the far side of the room. "That's a wonderful piece. Where'd you find it?"

Her smile relaxed. "I got that at an estate sale a couple of years ago. I liked that it looked so...*used.* Like it has a history." She leaned back against the counter and swiped at a strand of hair. "I felt I didn't just *buy* it—it was more as if I'd *adopted* it."

Once she'd started talking, he'd let his focus once again drift up to her face, so animated and serene at the same time. A mistake, he quickly realized. The minute she caught his eye, the nervousness returned. When he took her hand, he felt her fingers quivering even as they closed around his. Then she snatched her hand away, shaking her head, and he knew the thread of her control was about to snap.

"Oh, Spencer..." Her voice had cracked. He saw her fight to regain her poise, but then, on a gulp of air, she lifted her hands to her face and dissolved into tears.

He quickly found a place to put down his glass and pulled her into his arms, nestling her head underneath his chin as he stroked her hair, feeling her tears soak into his shirt. "Shh, honey...it's okay, it's okay..." She felt so good cradled against him that it nearly took his breath away. "I know. We have a problem."

She sighed and wiped at her eyes with the back of her hand. "No. *I* have a problem."

He hooked her chin in his hand and tilted her face up to his, letting himself drown in the most beautiful, wettest, green-gray eyes in the world. "You're not alone, sweetheart. Not anymore."

Tears brimming again over her lower lashes, she slipped away from him and faced the sink, her hands braced on the front of the counter. Her only response was to shake her head.

Spencer sighed, moving beside her. "Look, obviously I don't know the details of how you got into this situation. But from what I know about you, it's a pretty good guess that some jerk is to blame. Not you." When she half turned to him, he added, "Mother told me yesterday that she's known for a couple of weeks." He reached over and brushed back another strand of hair that had fallen over her cheek. "I was ready to chew her out for not telling me sooner."

Several seconds passed, then she said, "She had guessed. I made her promise not to tell you. I—I didn't want you to know."

With a frown, he pulled her to him again, wrapping his arms around her slender waist, a waist that he well knew wouldn't stay that way much longer. "Why not?"

"Would it have made a difference?"

"It might have."

She gave him an unsteady smile, her long golden lashes spiked with tears. "And what would you have done? What *could* you have done? Besides, you were on the other side of the world…"

"I'd like to have been given the chance to find out…"

Her hands rested on his chest, so lightly he could barely feel them. "Oh, Spencer…this has nothing to do with you. I didn't—*don't*—want you to feel sorry for me."

He smiled down into her face. "Oh, believe me, I don't feel sorry for you."

The eyebrows lifted, but only slightly. Her gaze, though, met his dead-on. "Then…what do you feel for me?"

"Only this..."

He covered her mouth with his, resisting the urge to hold her as tightly as he wanted to for fear of frightening her, if not crushing her. In spite of her height, she felt as fragile as a snowflake in his arms as their tentative kiss grew deeper, more importunate the longer they stood there. A rushing warmth enveloped him when she timidly looped her arms around his neck, then let her fingers glide up into his hair. He broke the kiss, stroking her face in wonder for only a second before repossessing her mouth, desperate for completeness, desperate that she understand his need for her.

But with a little choked gasp, Brianna pushed away, her arms crossed protectively over her chest. "No," she said, shaking her head, and he cringed at the fear he heard in her voice.

He tried to reach out to her, but she retreated into the living room. He followed her, pleading. "Brianna—please don't think...I have no intention of acting like...whoever put you in this position..."

"I can't go through this again," she said, seemingly to herself.

"Can't go through what, sweetheart?"

She lifted an anguished, tear-streaked face to him and shook her head, the gesture ending in a shaky little sigh.

"Brianna..." He ached for what she must be feeling, but somehow knew he needed to be very careful about touching her again. "Honey, I don't want to have an affair with you. I want to *marry* you."

He saw her hands knot into fists. "You want to *what?*"

"Marry you. Spend the rest of my life with you." He crossed the floor to her, tentatively putting his hands on her shoulders. "Help you raise this baby."

"Don't be absurd—"

"That was not my intention."

Her eyes widened, disbelieving. "For crying out loud, Spencer—we barely know each other...and I am not interested in a marriage of convenience—"

He tightened his grip on her shoulders and held his face close to hers.

"Believe me—you're hardly what I'd call *convenient*, now are you?"

After a moment, she let out a short, sad laugh. "I guess you have a point."

"Damn straight." He took a deep breath and cupped the side of her face in his hand, stroking her wet cheek with his thumb. Her pulse beat gently at the base of her neck; he let the tops of his fingers find that soft throb, wanted to kiss her again. "The first time I met you, you resurrected feelings that I thought were long dead. That I thought I wanted to remain dead." He sighed, running his hands up and down her delicate arms. "You scared the hell out of me."

Another tight little laugh escaped from her throat. "Well, that's a new one. I've never been known to instill terror in grown men before." After a long pause, she added, "And now?"

He smiled and touched the tip of her nose with his finger. "You *still* scare the hell out of me. But I'm learning to enjoy it."

She gave him a shaky smile in return, then he saw her face cloud over as she shook her head for a moment before resting it against his chest. "I can't possibly marry you and you know it."

"I know no such thing. Why on earth not?"

"Oh, Spencer..." Her head came up swiftly, her eyes melting into his. "Think about it. How would it look? That you broke your engagement to Charlotte, then turned right around and walked down the aisle with me? God knows, Charlotte would probably cast some sort of voodoo spell on me. And I can't say that I'd blame her. Even if I weren't pregnant, it would be awkward. As I am..." She pushed her shoulders up into a helpless shrug.

He tightened his hold around her waist. "You really think I give a damn about any of that?"

She sighed. "Maybe not at the moment. Though I'm sure

you will, sooner or later. But whether you do or not, *I* do. I've gotten myself into a royal mess, I'll grant you that, but I'm hardly going to let myself be rescued. Especially in such a public way.'' She looked into his eyes, her own harboring an unlikely mix of apprehension and determination. ''I couldn't live the rest of my life having your society friends titter behind my back about the unconventional circumstances of our marriage. It wouldn't be fair to either of us.'' After a pause, she added, ''Or to the child.''

''That's ridiculous, Brianna, and you know it. People get married under 'unconventional', as you put it, circumstances, every day.''

''True. But they're not internationally known figures, Spence. I'm really not in the mood to land on the front page of some tabloid.''

''That won't happen....''

''Oh, and you can guarantee that?'' She grimaced. ''I don't think so. Besides—why on earth would you want to be father to a child that's not even yours?''

Spencer gently held Brianna back from his embrace and sought her eyes. ''Because the baby's *yours*. Because it will have your intelligence, and beauty, and wisdom...''

She pulled away from him and shook her head, walking over and sitting against the arm of the sofa, idly fingering the crocheted afghan draped across the back. ''Right. Wisdom is definitely one of my strong suits.''

He rubbed the side of his face, then sighed. ''So you made an error in judgment. I'm offering you a chance to correct it.''

The eyes expanded again. ''By marrying you? As if that somehow is going to fix everything—''

''Dammit, Brianna—I love you!''

She seemed to contemplate this for several seconds, then turned her gaze toward the open window, her voice quiet and wondering. ''You're still as arrogant and patronizing as you were the day you came into the salon, aren't you?''

''Brianna, please—if that's how you're reading this...'' This was *exactly* what he dreaded. Feeling helpless and frustrated and like a complete idiot. But what choice did he have? "Baby, I'm not trying to fix things, or save you, or whatever it is you think I'm trying to do. I know it won't be easy, no matter what path we take. I want to marry you for one reason only and that's because I love you. I just want to be with you and help you in any way you'll let me. Why can't you understand that?"

"Because this is my problem, not yours," she said quietly. Then, she regarded him again, her features now almost too calm, too composed. "Besides," she continued, "this may come as a surprise, but don't you think I might just be the slightest bit confused as to why you asked someone else to marry you when you yourself admitted that you were attracted to me?"

Spencer raked his hand through his hair, feeling as though he was walking a tightrope over Niagara Falls. "I haven't sorted that one out myself yet, not completely. Except that, I don't know..." He sighed. "I felt an obligation to Charlotte, and I was scared."

Her mouth crooked up on one side. "So you said. Of me."

"More than you." He walked over to the middle window and stared out over her backyard. "Did...my mother ever mention Barbara?"

She seemed to hesitate before answering. "No."

He glanced at her over his shoulder. She had slipped down into the corner of the sofa, her legs tucked under her, one finger scraping ridges in the nap of the velveteen upholstery. "No, of course she wouldn't," he said. "If there's one thing Mother's not, it's indiscreet." He hesitated, wondering how to talk about something he hadn't even allowed himself to *think* about for years.

"So...who is Barbara?"

"She was the only other woman that even came close to making me feel the way you do."

"Oh..."

The one word conveyed sadness, and understanding. And

something more. *Knowing.* He looked at her, his eyebrows pulled down. "You do know about this, don't you?"

"Yes, a little." She gave him a hint of a smile, and he would have forgiven her anything. "Kelly told me, in New York. She swore me to secrecy."

"Like you did with Mother?"

"Something like that, yes." He still couldn't read her expression. "Don't be too upset."

He shrugged. "It doesn't matter anymore. As I said, it was a long time ago. I was very young. She was even younger." He rubbed the back of his neck. "She dumped me. Left me standing at the altar. But I suppose you know that."

"Yes..." Brianna had wrapped her arms around herself. "But it's not the same as hearing you say it." She lifted her face to him. "What happened to her, do you know?"

With a shrug, he said, "I haven't a clue. She just vanished. But the term 'gun-shy' does not even come close to describe my attitude toward women for the next several years." He touched the filmy curtain beside him just as a puff of air plucked it out of his fingers. "I didn't think I was capable of loving again. Didn't want to. Then I met you... But the thought of opening myself up that way again..." He couldn't explain.

"I see," Brianna said softly. She stood and joined him at the window, her hands clasped behind her back. To keep from reaching out to him? he wondered. "And...how does Charlotte fit into all of this?" she asked.

She was near enough that he could smell her hair conditioner, as fresh as the spring air that suffused the apartment. "If I live to be a hundred," he admitted, "I'll never completely understand how that happened. I just know I came damn close to making a colossal mistake." He studied her as she stood so close to him, yet so purposefully distant, anguished that he couldn't tell what she was thinking.

He let his attention drift back out the window, ignoring the feeling in his gut that told him that things might not go his way.

"That night in New York, when we kissed..." On a sigh, he corrected himself. "Oh, hell, *before* we kissed, I knew then what I felt for you, but I simply couldn't handle it. I felt as if the rug had been pulled out from under me. Rotten excuse, I know. But I couldn't stand feeling so unstable, so out of control of my own destiny. Then Charlotte broached the subject of marriage. And in my panicked state I saw marriage to her as a safety net. As if, by committing myself to someone I didn't love, I would somehow stop loving you." He turned back to enigmatic eyes. "Coward's way out, huh?"

Brianna's laugh startled him. "I'd hardly qualify becoming engaged to Charlotte as being *cowardly.*"

Hoping that her laugh meant her mood—and the tide of the conversation—had changed, Spencer put his arm around her, carefully as if she were some wild thing that would dash away if he moved too quickly. "Perhaps you're right, now that I think about it."

She didn't lean into him, but neither did she pull away while he gently stroked her shoulder and neck as he watched the side of her face. The pregnancy had filled her out a bit, making her a little less fragile-looking but even prettier. He wanted to see her face in all its expressions—content, sad, worried, excited. Then he longed to know how she'd look at him when they made love. With a suppressed sigh, he wondered how on earth he'd managed to fall in love with a pregnant woman. But...he'd face anything, *anything,* as long as he could make her his.

"Brianna?"

"Hmm?"

He wondered where her thoughts had been. "At the risk of sounding presumptuous again...do you love me?"

She met his eyes after a moment, hers so full of pain he inwardly gasped. After several seconds, she whispered, "With all my heart."

"Then?"

"I'm so sorry. I can't marry you, Spence." She put two soft fingers on his lips to silence his objection, her eyes glistening with tears. "I didn't say I didn't want to," she said, her voice choked. "I said I *can't*."

He held her gaze for only a second. "Then there's no point in any further discussion, is there?" Hardly able to breathe for the pressure inside his chest, he pulled his arm from her shoulder and walked out the door.

Brianna jabbed a hole into the soil with her trowel, trying to convince herself as she sobbed that she wasn't a complete numbskull for refusing Spencer's proposal. No matter how much she tried to rationalize her decision, she couldn't shake off the nagging feeling that she'd just turned down Prince Charming. She didn't even attempt to dry her eyes when she heard the crunch of Zoe's car on the pebbled driveway twenty minutes later—she simply no longer cared who knew what. Especially Zoe.

She heard the car door slam shut, the sound of sneakers grinding in gravel as Zoe approached. "Hey, those petunias are going to look terrif— Whoa, lady! *What* is wrong with you?" She crouched beside Brianna, laying her hand on her shoulder.

With a feeble laugh, Brianna sat back on her knees and took out a tissue from her pocket, loudly blowing her nose. "Well, I guess it's time to let the cat—or in this case, *cats*—out of the bag." She huffed out a rattling sigh. "I'm pregnant."

The girl's lower jaw sank three inches. "You're *what?*"

"You heard me."

"How far…"

"Three months."

Her assistant swore under her breath. Then, "Wait a minute—you said *cats*. I'm afraid to ask—what else?"

"I also just declined Spencer Lockhart's marriage proposal."

Brianna thought Zoe's eyes would pop right out of her head.

"*That's* who got you pregnant?"

"Oh, no, no, no," she said, laughing in spite of herself at Zoe's expression.

"Believe it or not, the two things are not related. Exactly."

Zoe gaped at her, shaking her head. As she moved to sit on the bottom porch step, she said, "I am totally blown away." Then she smacked her forehead with the palm of her hand. "God, what an airhead. It never even *occurred* to me that you were so sick every morning a while back because you were *pregnant*..."

"You knew I was sick?"

"Oh, puh-lease, don't tell me you thought you were hiding it? We all noticed. But no one had the nerve to ask." Her mouth quirked up on one side. "Though I bet the older ladies had their suspicions. I guess no one wanted to mention what they were thinking to anyone else. I mean, you just don't go around surmising that your single boss is pregnant, you know?"

"Didn't seem possible?"

"Didn't seem *likely,* is more like it. I mean, you never even dated."

Brianna managed a wry smile, wondering when Zoe would click in. "Thanks for noticing."

Then Zoe gasped. "Except once. Oh, God—it's *Zimmerman's* baby, isn't it?"

Brianna nodded, then drew her mouth into a straight line. "I just have one thing to say, in case you're wondering. Actually, two things. One, you *can* get pregnant from just one encounter. And two, never believe a man when he tells you he's had a vasectomy unless he shows you an affidavit from his doctor."

"Uh...Brianna..." Zoe rested her head in her hand and slanted her a bemused look. "I don't know how to tell you this...but, like, I know that."

Brianna sighed. "Of course you would. Everybody would. Except me..."

"Hey, lady—don't you dare go beating yourself up over this. Where's Mr. Daddy-Man in all this?"

"I imagine he's at home with his wife and three kids."

"Oh..."

Brianna tapped a plant out of its container and stuck it in the ground. "Yeah...*oh*."

Zoe shook her head. "Still..." Then leaned her cheek in her hand. "God, you've got guts. You're going to raise this kid by yourself?"

"Apparently so."

"You happy about it?"

"The truth? At first, I was too stunned to be happy. But the old Responsibility Mode kicked in, so I just decided to deal with it." She looked over at the young woman. "The law may have given me several options, but my heart only left me with one."

"Yeah," Zoe said, squinting into the sun for a moment. "I can understand that."

"You do?"

"Yep." She nodded in the direction of Brianna's tummy. "Does it move yet?"

Brianna rubbed her abdomen, just beginning to swell at thirteen weeks. "Not yet. It's still early."

Then her assistant burst into a huge smile. "Can I be Auntie Zoe?"

"You sure can," Brianna managed to say over the lump in her throat.

Suddenly Zoe seemed to notice the masses of flowers on the porch steps and jumped to her feet. "Let me help you get these plants in the ground."

"I thought you came over to catch up on paperwork."

"Eh—it'll wait. It always does."

Brianna smacked an extra trowel into the girl's hand. "Far be it from me to turn down an extra pair of hands. Can I pay you with lunch?"

Zoe shrugged and picked up a six-pack of impatiens. "No argument here. Hey—" She grinned at Brianna. "Is it true that pregnant ladies are obsessed with food?"

Brianna wiped her face with the back of her hand and said on a rush of air, "Let's just say at the rate I'm going, this baby's going to weigh at least twenty pounds."

"You'll notice, I've been very good."

Brianna acknowledged Zoe's comment with a smirk as they sat with sweating glasses of lemonade on her porch. The flowers were all in, and the temperature had gotten high enough to make staying in the sun uncomfortable. Brianna pulled at the front of her jumper where perspiration had made it stick. "You've been very good about what?"

Zoe sipped her lemonade. "Asking you about Mr. Lockhart."

"Ah." Brianna shrugged, trying to look nonchalant when in fact Zoe's question had had the effect of pitchforking her heart. "I don't know that's there's much to say."

"The man asked you to marry him. Methinks there's a *little* more to this than you're admitting."

"Yes, well…" Brianna stared at her lemonade, feeling her heartbeat throb in her ears.

"Why'd you say no?"

"Why do you think?" Brianna placed her hand on her middle.

Zoe shook her head. "Bad reason. If the man's willing to marry you when you're pregnant with some other man's baby, doesn't that tell you something?"

"That he's lost his mind?"

"Oh, come off it, Brianna—no man proposes, no matter what the circumstances, unless he's lost his mind. That's a rule as unshakable as the law of gravity." Zoe stuck one finger in her lemonade and twirled the ice cubes. "You love him?"

Brianna felt her throat catch. All she could do was nod.

Zoe sighed. "Then *you're* one who's lost her mind."

Now it was Brianna's turn to sigh. "It's not that simple, Zoe. Look at his position. And he's been engaged…."

"*Been?* Then…he broke up with Demon Woman? *Yes!*"

"Now, Zoe…"

"Oh, don't *Now, Zoe* me. Charlotte Westwood is a witch and you know it. I'm sorry, but if the fiancée is out of the picture, I don't see the problem—"

"It just doesn't look good."

The young woman gawked at her. "What century did you grow up in, lady? *Doesn't look good?*"

"I still have a little pride left, Zo—"

"And fat lot of good that's going to do you in about six months. Face it, Brianna. The deed is done. You might as well make the best of it, right?"

With a sigh, Brianna set her empty glass on a small glass table beside her. "Well, it's all a moot point, anyway. After I rejected his offer, the look in his eyes…" She propped one elbow on the armrest and let her cheek fall into her hand. "He'll probably never even speak to me again, Zoe. I know it."

"Oh, Mr. Lockhart…" Mrs. Morgan leaned her prodigious bosom on her desk as she lowered her voice. "Miss Westwood is in your office. I told her I didn't know when you'd be in, but she insisted she'd wait." The secretary pushed her glasses back up onto the bridge of her nose. "I hope that's all right."

Spencer frowned, thinking the last thing he needed after his disastrous morning with Brianna was having to face Charlotte. He patted his secretary on the shoulder as he passed her desk. "Don't think another thing about it, Alice." He threw her a knowing smile as he grasped the brass doorknob to his office. "You wouldn't be able to stop a typhoon, either."

Charlotte was standing in front of the picture window behind his desk, her fingers toying with a double strand of baroque pearls as she took in the Atlanta skyline. She turned, almost guiltily, when she heard Spencer enter.

"Mrs. Morgan said I could wait…" A smile flickered across her lips, then died.

"What do you want, Charlotte?"

His eyes narrowed as he watched her approach him, her figure displayed to full advantage in the tightly fitted black silk suit, the jacket's wide peplum fanning out around her hips in such a way that made her waist appear enticingly small, her bosom even fuller, her hips more round. She stopped two feet away, as if testing the waters.

"I thought maybe we could have lunch."

He shook his head and crossed to the bar, where he poured himself a glass of Perrier water. "Sorry—I have a luncheon appointment in fifteen minutes." He backed against the bar with his hand in his pocket as he swirled the bubbly water around the glass with the other. "If you have something to say, you'll have to do it now."

She licked her lips as the nervous smile made another phantom appearance. "Okay...I guess I'll take whatever time I can get. I just want to...to apologize for my behavior the other night, at the restaurant? And to beg you to give me another chance."

"Charlotte, there's no point..."

She leaned back against his desk, her fingers skimming the edge as she talked. "At least, go with me to Allison Franklin's wedding on Saturday. It's a big affair, and if I show up alone..." She let her voice fade, bringing her left hand up to her collarbone.

Spencer's hand tightened around his glass as a flash of light caught his attention. The ring. He'd completely forgotten that Charlotte still wore the engagement ring he'd given her shortly after they'd come back from the weekend in New York. As far as she was concerned, he realized with a start, the engagement was still valid as long as she wore its symbol.

Then he thought of his futile conversation with Brianna a few hours ago, of the deaf ear she had turned to him, no matter how he tried to overcome her objections. *I can't marry you,* she had said.

He was angry. And hurt. And completely baffled by her behavior.

And he knew she was doing Allison Franklin's wedding.

He let his gaze drift out the window for a moment, then dragged it back to find Charlotte's entreating, glistening eyes fixed on him. Brown eyes.

Not hazy green.

"In case you missed something, Charlotte," he said dispassionately. "We broke up. If you want to go to Allison's wedding, you'll either have to go by yourself or find another escort.''

He watched with some satisfaction as Charlotte's face reddened to nearly the color of her lips. Then, wordlessly, she yanked her purse off his desk and swept past him out of the office.

9

Brianna nearly knocked the phone off the nightstand when it shrilled.

"H-hello?" She pushed her hair out of her face and tried to focus on the clock. Six-fourteen. "Yes? Okay...okay... calm down, Mrs. Franklin." She pressed her hand against the air in front of her as if the overwrought mother could see the gesture. "Now...what's this?"

She twisted herself around and pushed aside the lace curtain. Gray and gloomy. Just wonderful. In the middle of a yawn, she sat bolt upright.

"You're kidding? No, he didn't call me... Yes, of course he was supposed to..."

But then, not even the birds are up yet, Mrs. Franklin.

"No...please don't worry. As long as all the food's there, we'll just all pitch in and help... Of course, I'll come early... Yes, I promise." She paused. "Is Allison awake yet?... No?... Well, good for her... No, please, don't tell her anything...The weather?" She peered out the window again. "Oh, it'll probably clear up. Just a predawn haze, I'm sure." She smiled into the phone. "I wish I could, Mrs. Franklin. But just think how much more expensive I'd be if I could guarantee the weather, on top of everything else! Okay, you go have a cup of coffee, and I'll see you later."

She hung up and collapsed back against her pillows with another loud yawn. The ceremony wasn't until four, the reception six. Plenty of time...

She sat up and immediately dialed Zoe.

"Yeah, I know what time it is. Sorry. Listen, you're not going to believe this. *Both* of Marcel's assistants called in sick this morning. Look's like we're going to have to pinch hit... No, I haven't spoken to him yet. Apparently he called Mrs. Franklin first... I have no idea why. But then, Marcel works in mysterious ways, as we all know... I don't know. About ten, I guess... Of course I'm okay, silly.... Okeydoke, I'll see you then."

As she hung up the second time, it started to pour as if someone had ripped open a zipper in the clouds.

Brianna wondered if she'd missed hearing about the hurricane that had obviously moved into Atlanta overnight. She'd never seen it rain this hard, anywhere, anytime. The windshield wipers on the van as good as useless, it took an hour and a half to wend her way to Vinings, at the far northwest corner of the city, from the salon in the center of town. When she at last arrived at the Franklins home, her jeans—which she now had to leave unbuttoned at the waistband—and oversize T-shirt were saturated with moisture. Zoe greeted her in the mudroom with rolling eyes.

"The bride is in hysterics, the mother is in hysterics, and Marcel is not to be believed, in spite of what I brought him."

"Oh?" Brianna asked, trying to find someplace to prop her dripping umbrella. "And what, exactly, did you bring him?"

"Auntie Rose and Cousin Sheila," she said, leading Brianna through the adjacent mudroom into the kitchen.

"You brought *relatives?*"

"Yeah, well—at least they're bodies, right?"

"Oh, thank you, kind girl!" Brianna threw her arms around Zoe, almost immediately pushing her back to arm's length. "I take it these particular bodies were chosen for their culinary skills, right?"

"Yeah—those two can chop, dice, and arrange with the best of 'em. As long as Marcel understands that Rose doesn't speak much English..."

"Tell me you're kidding."

"Nope. Hey—lighten up. As long as Sheila stays by her to translate, everything'll be just fine."

Brianna glanced around the restaurant-size kitchen as if searching for a land mine, offering a smile for the two Chinese-American ladies seated at the breakfast bar. They nodded and smiled simultaneously in return. "Uh, where *is* Marcel?" she whispered.

Zoe raised her eyebrows. "I don't know. He was here a minute ago."

Brianna shut her eyes for a moment, trying to restore her breathing to normal. She felt Zoe's hand on her forearm and opened her eyes.

"You okay?"

Brianna frowned. "You're going to ask me that at least five hundred times between now and October fifteenth, aren't you?"

"Probably." The black eyes glistened. "That's when it's due? You hadn't told me."

Brianna nodded.

"Neat."

"We're off the subject."

"Right. Marcel." Zoe shrugged. "I haven't a clue. In the john?"

"God, let's hope…"

"Miss Fairchild—thank *God* you're finally here!" Delia Franklin flew down the back staircase into the kitchen, clutching closed a pink satin kimono to her breasts, her hair held hostage by a dozen orange-juice-can-size rollers. "The flowers!"

"What about the flowers?" This was not going to be good news.

"The truck got into an accident coming out here…."

"Oh, my God!" Brianna had known the florist since she started. "Is Jimmy all right?"

"Yes, yes, he called me from his car phone. But he had to wait for another van to come pick up the flowers and get them to the church and here. That means we're running at least an hour and a half behind schedule—''

Brianna shook her head, running her hand through her frizzing hair. "No, it doesn't."

Mrs. Franklin stopped in midsentence, the rollers quivering on top of her head. "It doesn't?"

"No," Brianna smiled. "I always allow extra time for emergencies. The florist may have to hustle a little, but there's no disaster." She touched Mrs. Franklin's shoulder, attempting to sound much more calm than she felt. "Did you ever get that cup of coffee?"

"No…"

"Then, please—go have one now. Everything's just fine. Really."

Just keep telling yourself that, she thought.

"Okay, Zoe," she said, warily eyeing Mrs. Franklin as she shuffled across the kitchen toward the coffeepot. "I guess we face Allison next?"

"I already have, remember?" She pretended to bow. "You may have the honors."

They found a pajama-clad Allison huddled in front of her skirted vanity in her pink-and-lavender childhood bedroom, clutching an old teddy bear. Even Brianna had to feel a twinge of sympathy for the young woman when she saw her tear-streaked face and quivering lower lip.

"Oh, Miss Fairchild! This is *horrible!*" She threw herself sobbing into Brianna's arms. "It's p-pouring c-cats and d-dogs, my hair has *never* looked so awful, and I'm so nervous I'm r-ready to k-kill anyone who looks at me the w-wrong way!"

Brianna moved Allison over to sit on the canopied bed, stroking her riot of auburn curls and soothing her as if she were a little child.

"Hey—have you heard from Robert yet?"

Allison shook her head and reached around to grab a tissue, honking for all she was worth into it. "N-no." Her eyelids were so red and puffy Brianna could hardly see her eyes. "It's bad luck to see the g-groom before the wedding, remember?"

Brianna laughed. "To *see* him, not *talk* to him, silly. Why don't you give him a call? I bet he's feeling like a bowl of Jell-O right about now himself."

"Not Robert. *Nothing* bothers him."

Brianna thought about the quiet young surgeon who was about to plight his troth to the hysterical woman in her arms. Yes, under normal circumstances, she'd bet Robert Worthington was pretty unflappable. But this was his wedding day. She'd not yet met a groom who wouldn't have preferred dental surgery to getting married.

"Why don't you give him a call, anyway? I bet you'll both feel better."

Allison lifted her face, her red-rimmed eyes hopeful. "You think?"

"I *know.*" Brianna patted her on the back. "And when you're finished, we'll get you into a nice hot bath and then get some breakfast into you…"

"Oh, no—I couldn't eat anything…"

"I'm sure we can get tea and toast down your gullet, young woman. I will not have you fainting from hunger once you get that gown on."

Allison's face fell two stories. "Oh, my God—the dress! It's pouring! How'm I going to get to the church in the dress—"

"You think you're the only woman who ever got married when it was raining?" Zoe interjected with a wide grin. "This is why plastic dress bags were invented. We double bag the gown, get it over to the church early, steam it out, and dress you there. So maybe you don't make the big entrance up the church steps in the gown, but, hey—at least you'll be dry, right?"

The brows plunged. "I don't know…"

Brianna took her by the shoulders and looked her in the eye. "Allison, listen to me." She kept a practiced balance between firmness and affection in her tone. "It's raining. We

can't change that. So we adapt. It's what ensures the survival
of the species, remember? If the sun comes out, you dress
here. If it keeps raining, you'll dress at church. Really—it's
no big deal.''

The bride managed a little laugh. ''I guess you're right.''
Then she said, ''At least, it's not as if the caterer's disappeared
or anything, right?''

Brianna didn't dare look at Zoe.

Twelve noon. It was raining even harder, if that was possible, moisture penetrating every corner of the house, the constant drumming on the flagstone patio outside the kitchen driving Brianna crazy.

At least Marcel was in residence, in a supreme snit, as if
the weather was a personal insult. His temper was so foul he
could only allow a grudging ''thank you'' to Zoe's aunt and
cousin, which irritated the life out of the tired, hungry, and
clammy Brianna.

She had watched the thin, coffee-colored arms flail pots and
pans and serving trays around the kitchen for twenty minutes,
as the caterer complained about the stove, the refrigerator, the
lighting, the layout. Finally, Brianna slammed down a cookie
sheet onto the island, making the two little ladies jump a foot.

''That's *enough*, Marcel. Knock it off, will you?''

Marcel planted one hand on his hip and glared at her.
''Well, excuse me, but if I don't like the facilities, I think I
have every right to voice my complaints.''

''There's not a damn thing wrong with this kitchen, and
you know it,'' Brianna retorted, leaning over the island toward
him. ''In fact, you said so yourself when we previewed the
facilities a month ago. Everything is professionally sized and
in perfect working order. So get over it. You're upsetting your
assistants with your infantile behavior.''

It was the wrong thing to say, but she didn't care.

''My *assistants?*'' Marcel said with a sneer. ''Those two?
And just how am I supposed to use two women who don't
have a clue as to how I work, hmm?''

Out of the corner of her eye, Brianna could see the younger woman rapidly translating their conversation to the older one, whose eyes were becoming larger with every additional exchange.

"Fine, Marcel. So do it all yourself. Either that, or learn to cope, for crying out loud." She straightened and crossed her arms. "God knows I pay you enough to be a little flexible."

Marcel pursed his too thin lips and rolled his eyes. "Pay me enough? Oh, don't get me started—"

"No—don't get *me* started!" Brianna snapped at him, feeling her face grow warm. "I know exactly what you were getting for a job before I came on the scene. Those other consultants paid you squat, and you know it. But you were—are—the best caterer in town, so I made sure you wouldn't work for anyone else by paying you twice as much as they would have. And with your attitude, you're lucky to work for *anyone*." She rammed her gaze into Marcel's dark chocolate eyes. "Now, get this straight. Either you get with the program and stop flitting around like a prima donna, or this will be the last time you work for me. Do you understand?"

He narrowed his eyes at her. "And just who do you think you're threatening, Miss High and Mighty? You've got a dozen weddings to do in the next month. Who're you going to get on such short notice?"

"I'll cook the food myself if I have to," she flung back, then pointed her finger at him. "And don't forget the clout I carry, buddy. If I no longer use your services, believe me, no one else will, either."

They stared each other down for a full ten seconds, then Marcel whipped around, walked over to Zoe's relatives, and began explaining what he wanted them to do.

Brianna felt the beginning of a headache as she released a tremendous sigh. The fight she had just had with Marcel was not much different from the one she had had with him just two weeks ago, and again the week before that. He seemed to work best after a good shouting match, like those hard-tofathom couples who made the best love after a heated argument. She just wasn't up for the stress, not today.

Wearily rubbing the base of her spine in a futile attempt to relax a cramped muscle, she went off to check on the floral situation. In less than two hours, she would have to be dressed and at the church.

She peeked out at the mercilessly gray sky as she passed by a window and swore under her breath.

"Jeez, Brianna—are you all right?"

She and Zoe were getting dressed in one of the guest rooms, standing side by side in front of the vanity mirror. Brianna shot a warning glance at her assistant's reflection.

Zoe stuck out her tongue as she hitched up her panty hose underneath her turquoise silk dress. "No, I mean it. I don't like the way you look." She zipped up the back of Brianna's dress, a dropped-waist pale yellow silk chiffon that fell to midcalf. "Did you ever get anything to eat today?"

Brianna smiled and clipped on a pair of pearl and rhinestone earrings, then smoothed back a few errant strands into her French twist. "Whatever I could snatch from the kitchen when Marcel wasn't looking. Zoe, I'm pregnant, I'm tired, and it's been a helluva day. And the wedding isn't for another two hours yet. I'm entitled."

The younger woman shook her head, unconvinced. Then she gave a little gasp. "There is a God. Look!"

"What?"

"On the floor! What is that?"

Brianna's eyes followed a silver-ringed finger to a patch of sunlight on the gleaming wood floor.

Dazed, they both looked out the bedroom window.

There wasn't a cloud to be seen.

The church was far too small for several hundred guests, but it was so quaint and pretty that no one minded. Brianna could just imagine wedding-goers from another era pulling up in front of the ivy-covered dark red brick structure in their hansom carriages. However, the parking lot was filled instead with Mercedes and BMWs and Caddies, with an occasional Toyota or Range Rover thrown in for variety.

The majority of the guests were already seated when Brianna heard the rumble of approval from latecomers, as well as attendees who had hung back on purpose just to see *the dress*, as Allison arrived. With a calm nod, she signaled to the organist to begin the prelude, then slipped out a side door, bridal bouquet in hand, and down the hall to the vestibule.

Zoe had ushered the bride and her stoic father as far out of the way of the flow of guests still straggling in as she could, but the enormous dress—not to mention twelve twittering bridesmaids in a rainbow of frothy organza—still filled up nearly half of the tiny vestibule.

"Well, lady, what d'ya think?" Zoe asked her employer over the cacophony of high-pitched female voices as she busied herself with straightening yards and yards of rumpled taffeta and beaded lace.

"No," Brianna replied. "The question is, what does the *bride* think?"

Allison answered with a radiant smile, nodding or giving a tiny wave now and then at someone she recognized passing through the lobby. "I couldn't be happier, Miss Fairchild," she giggled, prettier than Brianna had ever seen her. "And you can't tell me you didn't have anything to do with making the sun come out! In fact, I told Daddy to give you a big bonus for it!"

Mr. Franklin's only comment was a grunt and a roll of his eyes as he tugged at his too tight cummerbund.

The day had finally decided to cooperate. Marcel was under control, all the flowers were in place at both locations, the rain had disappeared, and the bride was breathtaking. Chuckling, Brianna maneuvered her way around to Allison's back to fiddle with her headpiece and veil, only to feel her hands go ice cold as her ears picked out a familiar, deep male voice in the crush. One of the bridesmaids planted herself in her face and whined, "Miss Fairchild, I think my headpiece should be further down, don't you?"

She barely heard the bridesmaid's question, or Zoe's quick reply, or any of the hundred other noises in the vestibule at that moment. She was only aware that the man whose proposal of marriage she had recently refused was standing not four feet in front of her. And next to him, barely wearing an expensive strapless dress in a swirling print of hot turquoise and fuchsia and red-orange jungle flowers, stood the very woman he was supposedly no longer engaged to, the ostentatious solitaire diamond still flagrantly in evidence on her claw-nailed left hand.

"Oh, my God, Allison!" Charlotte oozed. "You look absolutely *gorgeous!* Doesn't she, Spencer, darlin'?"

Before Brianna had a chance to think, their eyes locked, for no more than a second. Just long enough for her to see a thousand emotions flash through his, for hers to fill up with tears.

"Well, Allison—you're all ready!" Brianna forced her voice to sound bright, cheerful. She lowered her head to Zoe. "If you don't mind..."

"Go on," her assistant whispered. "Get out of here."

Gratefully, Brianna nodded, then slipped back into the side passageway, leaning against the wall with her hand pressed to her mouth as the organist played the first notes of the Purcell processional.

Damn Charlotte!
Like a cat stalking a mouse, she had waited until he showed up, then sidled up to him in the last-minute throng so that everyone who saw them would assume they were together.

Timed it just perfectly so that *Brianna* would see them together.

The pain in her eyes had devastated him. He sat through the wedding service, unhearing, unseeing, unable to think of anything but how tired and unhappy Brianna seemed.

And how much he ached to hold her in his arms.

To explain.

Anything he might have done to extricate himself from Charlotte's clutches would have more than likely brought on a scene. Not something a Southern gentleman allowed to happen on someone's wedding day, that was for sure. So he'd decided to let her have her moment, then slip away from her once inside the church. What he hadn't counted on was the scarcity of seats in the church.

Or Charlotte's determination.

So here she sat, plastered next to him in that blinding dress, her brow arched just slightly as she occasionally, casually, moved her left hand, the diamond flashing like a spotlight each time she did. He thought of the hundreds of business deals he'd negotiated, bargaining tables at which he'd mediated, union leaders with whom he'd come to terms. Never, not once, had he ever had any doubts about his ability to set straight a business course that had gone awry. But give him a woman—or worse, two women—to deal with, and he was lost.

The ring's sparkle caught his eye as Charlotte shifted ostentatiously in her seat.

Feeling the muscles in his face converge into an award-winning scowl, he crossed his arms and wondered when the next Train to Hell left the station.

Delia Franklin grabbed Brianna by the arm and pulled her over to the kitchen window. "Would you look at that? We always called her our princess, but now I think it's really true."

Brianna wiped a bit of pâté off her fingers onto a paper towel and followed Mrs. Franklin's gaze out the window to a bank of outrageously profuse deep pink azaleas, in front of which her daughter and her new son-in-law stood with outrageously large smiles, having their photographs taken.

"Did you ever see anything more gorgeous?" Mrs. Franklin asked in a hushed voice.

"Nope," Brianna replied, then slanted a grin at her client. "Still won't play poker with me, Mrs. Franklin?"

"Not on your life." The woman laughed. "But you can sell us a bridal gown any day."

Allison had three younger sisters. Brianna laughed. "It's a deal. Now, I believe you have a party you're supposed to be attending?"

Mrs. Franklin nodded, her eyes glittering nearly as much as her silver cracked-ice chiffon gown. "Don't stay in here too long, darlin'. There's lots of folks out there I want you to meet." She winked. "Folks with daughters."

"I promise. I'll be out soon."

Unless I can possibly avoid it.

Still reeling after her encounter with Spencer at the church, Brianna had holed up in the kitchen, ostensibly to help the short-handed Marcel. Considering the atmosphere in the room, she wasn't sure she had made the best choice. But it was the only one she could think of.

"No, no, *no!* Little roses, I said! I want the radishes cut into…oh, hell, what's the use?" Marcel smacked a towel onto the counter and hooked his hand on his hip.

"What's wrong now, Marcel?" Brianna formed a perfect mound of pâté in the crystal serving dish and set it on another dish with overlapping bayleaves.

"Anybody ever teach these yahoos how to follow directions?"

Brianna scanned the dozens of dishes about to be set out on for the buffet in the dining room. They were gorgeous, even better looking than Marcel's usual spread.

Suddenly she understood.

"Why, you turkey—you're *jealous!*"

"I am not!"

"You are! Those ladies are doing a terrific job." She shook her head and sighed, leaning one hand on the island. "I really don't understand you, Marcel. You know everything's spectacular, and you know that you'll get the credit for it. My clients tip well, if they're pleased. And you know that, too." She looked up at him. "Maybe it's just because I'm so tired. Or because it's been such a rough day, I don't know. But either your contentious attitude goes, or you do. I meant what I said earlier.'' She placed the pâté with the other dishes and took off her apron. ''I just don't want to play this game anymore—''

''Allison hooked the gown on a branch after the photo session,'' a breathless Zoe announced as she burst into the kitchen. ''There's a big rip in the lace.''

''Big?'' Brianna asked, Marcel momentarily forgotten. Zoe was prone to exaggeration.

Zoe held her hands at least a foot apart.

Brianna sighed and held her hand to her head. ''Where's the sewing kit?''

''In the bedroom. Allison's in tears again.''

Brianna smiled wearily. ''Of course she is. She probably thinks it's all symbolic, that the fabric of her marriage had been torn asunder somehow because her lace is ripped—''

A car engine revved just outside the kitchen, followed by the sound of tires squealing in a hasty retreat. Zoe ran to the window, then turned to Brianna. Her complexion had gone slightly gray.

''That was Marcel.''

Brianna glanced around the kitchen as if there was a chance that her assistant was just playing a joke on her. As if she understood, Zoe shook her head. ''Now what?''

Quickly, Brianna cataloged the completed dishes already to go out on the buffet table, then checked the bulletin board Marcel always set up when he worked. ''From what I can tell from his chicken scratches, it's at least half done. The problem will be backup dishes.''

Zoe shrugged. ''We'll manage.''

''Oh, yeah? How good of a cook are you?''

''Me? I stink. But I never got the chance to tell you. Auntie Rose just moved to Atlanta from San Francisco to be nearer my mother.''

''Is there a point, Zo?''

''Guess what she did in San Francisco?''

"Zoe!"

With a huge grin, Zoe said, "She ran a catering business."

It took Brianna twenty minutes to stitch up the rip in Allison's dress and another twenty minutes to get her calmed down. By this time, she had decided that the events of the day put this affair solidly in the qualifying round for the Wedding from Hell for 1998. It would be at least midnight before she got out of there. Another five hours. For the first time since she'd started her business, she seriously considered jumping ship.

After showing Allison how to wrap her veil around her arm like a shawl so she could eat and dance, Brianna shooed her out the door, then fell into an armchair in the bedroom with her head thrown back.

She almost didn't hear the quiet knock.

Frowning, she pulled herself out of the chair. A bridesmaid searching for Allison, probably. She ran a hand over her hair and opened the door.

"Edwina!"

"Zoe told me you were up here." Brianna just stood aside and let the older woman into the room, who surveyed her with a dissatisfied expression as she passed. "She also told me she was worried about you. I can see why." She wagged a finger at her. "This is not good, Brianna. Not if you want a healthy baby."

Brianna smiled and sank back into the chair. "Today's been unusually fraught with complications, that's all. In a few hours it'll all be over and I'll go home and go to bed."

"And get up tomorrow and do it all over again?"

"Zoe's going out tomorrow. It's a smaller affair. I don't need to be there."

"Well, at least there's that." She paused. "Look, I know this is probably not the place to bring this up, but Spencer told me he'd proposed."

Brianna took in a small, sharp breath, then nodded.

"And that you'd turned him down."

All she could do was offer tear-filled eyes to the blue-gray ones focused on her face.

"Oh, honey—just look at you. *Why?*"

Brianna swallowed hard, trying to keep the tears at bay. Her success was minimal. "What's the point, Edwina? Or didn't you notice who he's here with tonight? Who's *still* wearing his engagement ring?"

She gave a terse nod, then said, "I can give you my word that that's one situation that will be alleviated by the end of the evening."

"Oh?" Brianna gave a shaky smile. "Are you planning on Charlotte having a little 'accident' or something?"

With a loud laugh, Edwina shook her head. "Lord—the dress alone would give me sufficient cause, don't you think? But no, even though it's very tempting." She studied Brianna's face for a moment, then said simply, "I know my son. He told me that Charlotte hadn't returned the ring, and he's too much of a damned gentleman to demand it back."

"That doesn't mean he had to bring her to the wedding, does it?"

Edwina threw her head back and howled with laughter. "Hell, he told her in no uncertain terms he wouldn't go with her. But when it comes to wily women, the man's as gullible as a pup."

"I...don't understand."

"Honey—she staged the whole thing. You should have seen Spencer by the time the wedding was over. That young woman's lucky to be *alive*." Her laughter died down as she said, "He was also extremely upset that you saw them together. Even though you'd turned him down."

Brianna lowered her head and stared at her hands, laced tightly together in her lap. She figured what was coming.

It came.

"So—as Charlotte's no longer a problem—?"

But Brianna just banged her knotted hands against her thighs. "I just can't saddle him with someone else's baby, with a woman so stupid as to let herself get pregnant—"

"Brianna!" Edwina barked, making her jerk up her head. The old woman's eyes flashed like blue lightening. "Don't you *ever* let me hear you refer to yourself that way again, do you hear me? There's not a creature on God's earth who hasn't screwed up occasionally. The only mistake, if there is one, is in not making the best of it. Besides, don't you think that's Spencer's decision to make?" She let out an aggravated sigh. "The two of you are just nuts about each other—"

Brianna rose from the chair, her weariness making her impatient. "Edwina, I'm extremely fond of you, and I appreciate your concern—"

"I know, I know—but please butt out." The older woman pushed herself up from the end of the bed and planted herself smack in front of Brianna. "I wish I could. Trouble is, I thought you'd make a perfect daughter-in-law the minute I laid eyes on you."

"You did?"

Edwina chuckled. "I'm sure you thought I was crazy for insisting you join us for dinner that night—"

"The thought crossed my mind, yes."

"I did it on purpose, you know. The whole mess needed to be brought to a head."

A puff of air escaped Brianna's lips. "Well, it certainly was. With a vengeance."

"But that's *good,* honey. There was no fixing the problem until that happened. I know you don't believe me, but it's true." She put her arm around Brianna's shoulder and gave her a firm squeeze. "You're perfect for each other, honey. And if he asks you to marry him again, for God's sake, say 'yes' this time, would you?"

If only it were that easy, Brianna thought as she gave a weak smile in reply.

There were far too many people in the house. After twenty minutes, the lack of air and incessant thrum of pointless small talk drove Spencer out onto the multilevel deck on the side of the house, then across the enormous yard toward a white gingerbreaded gazebo maybe a hundred feet away. Mauve twilight hung heavily in the air, waiting to drown the broad bands of peach and salmon and heliotrope that streaked the western sky. As he walked, he caught the occasional trill of a cricket revving up for its nightly serenade.

He swiftly negotiated the few steps of the wooden structure, his footsteps resounding against the hollow floor as he crossed to the opposite side in order to survey the immaculately kept grounds sweeping toward the west. The sultry early evening air pulsed with the heady fragrance of honeysuckle, petunias, roses—the same fragrance as at Brianna's, he realized, shutting his eyes against the ache.

"Spencer, darlin'? What on earth are you doing out *here?*"

He shifted to see Charlotte picking her way toward him through the wet grass, her full short skirt flouncing around her knees as she walked.

"Breathing," he said.

He'd thrown her with that one. But not for long. Drawing a flimsy scarf up over her bare shoulders, she joined him in the gazebo, her intentions clearly etched across her features.

Spencer watched, and waited, and decided to let her hang herself.

She stroked a finger over one of the wooden benches inside, then shook droplets of water from it. "Oh, pooh—it's still wet." Pivoting back to him, she cocked her head, a lazy smile spreading out her lips. "You know, you could kiss me." She took a step toward him, hitching her shoulders underneath the chiffon. "No one would see—"

"Charlotte, cut it out."

Undaunted, she sidled up to him, her hands demurely tucked behind her back so that the scarf slipped. "I promise I won't scream or slap your face or anything…"

Her hands floated up to his chest…but he cuffed her wrists before she made contact and firmly removed her hands to her sides.

"No."

He watched as the determination in those deep brown eyes

flared, then finally flickered out. She let her gaze linger for a long moment, then crossed to the other side of the gazebo with her arms once again folded behind her back. He heard a sigh, followed by a small, sad laugh. "Well, you can't blame a girl for trying."

Her head dropped as her hands disappeared in front of her for a moment. When she turned around, her right hand was extended, the engagement ring pinched between her thumb and forefinger as if it was on fire. "Please..." she said, her voice wobbling. "You'd better take this before I change my mind."

He hesitated, then held out his hand, an immense relief washing over him the instant he felt the cold metal and diamond drop into his palm. As he closed his fingers around it, he nodded. "Thank you." He looked up at her, saw she was trying not to cry. "I'm so sorry."

With another little laugh, she shook her head. "Don't be. I tried to force your hand. It didn't work, that's all." She shrugged. "Nobody can help what they feel."

She strolled to the other side of the gazebo and leaned her hands on the railing in spite of the dampness. As she scanned the grounds below them, she said quietly, "I saw your face today, when you caught sight of her in the church vestibule before the wedding. I knew then the battle was lost." After a moment she asked, "You absolutely adore her, don't you?" There was a sense of wonder in her voice that he'd never heard before.

Adore. More than love. He *adored* Brianna. Slipping the ring into his pocket, he answered Charlotte at last. "Yes. I really do."

Her fingers tightened their grip on the railing, then relaxed. "You going to marry her?"

"I don't know."

She twisted around, her eyebrows raised. In the dim light, he could barely see the incredulous smile on her lips. "You don't know?"

"She...she's *conflicted,* I believe is the correct term."

Charlotte seemed to consider this for a minute, then resumed her contemplation of the grounds. "Hell, she's just *nuts*, if you ask me."

Spencer chuckled quietly, remembering how likable Charlotte could be when she had a mind to. He leaned back against the railing and folded his arms across his chest. "How are you going to handle—"

"Calling off the wedding?" she finished. He saw her shoulders rise, then fall. "It's still six weeks away. The invitations haven't even gone out yet. I suppose we'll lose the deposits on the hall, and the florist, and the gown—"

"Please…" Spencer cut her off. "Don't think another thing about it. I'll make good on all of it. It's the least I can do."

For a second she didn't respond, then he saw her give a short nod.

They stood in silence for another minute, each on their own side of the filigreed structure. At last, Charlotte approached him again, but this time her gait and expression were completely guileless. She stopped a couple of feet in front of him, her arms loosely folded across her midriff. When she spoke, there was not a trace of anger in her voice, just a mild regret.

"You never should have agreed to marry me."

He unfolded his arms and rested his palms on the railing on either side of his hips. "Yeah. I know."

"And I should never have let it all get this far." She pulled the ineffectual scarf more tightly over her shoulders and inclined her head. "Neither of us would ever have been happy, would we?"

He regarded her in silence for a moment, then said quietly, "Especially you."

"Especially me," she echoed. She closed the space between them, placed one hand so lightly on his chest he could barely feel it, and brushed her lips against his cheek. When she pulled away, he saw her dark eyes shimmering with tears in the half light. "I won't say this doesn't hurt, because it does. But most of it's my doing. And I know I'll be fine. It's just…I'd like to go back inside, just for a little while longer. It's such a lovely party. Tomorrow, we'll announce that the engagement is off." She tossed her dark curls, then skipped down the steps. When she reached the lawn, she spun around, dancing backward toward the house. "Tonight, I just want to drink lots and lots of champagne!"

Spencer slowly followed, his brows knit so hard he nearly got a headache. As his hand found its way to the pocketed ring, he wondered how it was possible to feel such profound sadness and exhilaration at the same time.

Brianna waited another five minutes after Spencer's mother left the room before tentatively going downstairs to the reception. At last, everything seemed to going well. Several downstairs rooms were filled with laughter and eating and dancing; she received repeated compliments over the next hour as she passed from room to room.

"Oh, so *you're* Miss Fairchild! And you designed the dress? Why, that's the most beautiful gown I've ever seen..."

"Did you pick the music for the ceremony? It was wonderful..."

"Gorgeous flower arrangements...so unusual..."

"Where'd you get the idea for a Chinese buffet? This is the best wedding food I've had in years..."

"Why, Miss Fairchild! I do believe you've outdone yourself this time."

Brianna found herself face to face with Charlotte. And *only* Charlotte. "I'm glad you're enjoying it, Miss Westwood."

"Oh, honey, please...*Charlotte.*" Her giggles were too loud. Brianna's eyes automatically flicked to the champagne glass gripped in Charlotte's hand and she wondered how many like it there had been that evening. "And how is the little mother feeling tonight?"

Suddenly a little light-headed, Brianna shut her eyes for a moment, grateful for the din in the room. No one else could possibly have heard Charlotte.

"I'm fine," she said in a flat tone, opening her eyes again.

"I'm *so* glad to hear it..."

The dizziness became stronger, then passed. Brianna braced her hand on the buffet table and took a deep breath.

Then her knees gave way and the room spun around. She was vaguely aware of the clattering of a dish as it crashed to the floor, a splash of something wet across her arm, and then, just before everything went black, Spencer's low voice softly uttering her name in her ear as she crumpled against him on her way to the floor.

10

Dr. Steinberg removed the blood pressure cuff from Brianna's arm with a loud *wratch,* then tucked the apparatus neatly into her bag. "You know, the longer I do this, the more I'm amazed at how resilient the human species is. That little tyke inside you is just fine, in spite of how you treat yourself."

Brianna shifted against the mound of rose-and-white Laura Ashley print pillows behind her back and managed a wan smile as she sipped some orange juice. "You know I wouldn't knowingly do anything to hurt this baby...."

The doctor grunted, then squeezed Brianna's hand. "I know that, dear. But honestly—what you've been through today would fell a Sumo wrestler. I may be old fashioned, but in spite of everything you read, you can't do it all when you're pregnant. Carrying that baby is the most important thing you're doing right now."

Brianna nodded sheepishly. "I'm just glad you were nearby."

The doctor stood and smiled at her patient. "So am I. Now, all you need is food and rest. As I said, the baby's fine. You say you're not cramping, and there's no sign of bleeding, so that's that. Just stay off your feet for a few more minutes. And *eat* something, for God's sake!" She snapped shut her medical bag and asked, "Now, is this handsome man going to take you home soon?"

"Just as soon as she's ready to go," answered Spencer from the other side of the Franklins largest guest room. As he showed Dr. Steinberg out the bedroom door, Brianna leaned back against the pillows and sighed. She rolled her head and smiled as she felt the bed sag from Spencer's weight as he sat on its edge. It made no sense, but he was the only person she wanted there with her at the moment.

"You scared the hell out of me, lady," he said softly, taking her hand in his and rubbing his thumb over her knuckles.

Tears sprang to her eyes. Again. "I guess I have to stop doing that, huh?"

He smiled and kissed her fingers, then put her hand back on her lap. "That would be nice, yes." After several seconds he said, "I have something to show you."

Brianna lifted her eyebrows, questioning, then watched as Spencer slowly reached into his suit pocket and took something out, something that glittered in his palm as he held out his hand for her to see.

The engagement ring.

"*Now* do you believe me?" he asked.

Her heart went into overdrive. There was nothing between her and his proposal now except her resistance. And they both knew it.

She closed his fingers around the ring and pushed his hand away, then swung her legs around and lowered her stockinged feet into thick white carpeting. "Could we leave now?"

"Brianna, sweetheart, my offer still stands."

She faced those kind, deep blue eyes, then put her hand on his arm, rubbing the nubby silk of his jacket. "I know. But..."

"But. Always *but*—"

The rap on the door cut through their thoughts. "Hey, it's me. What're the two of you doing in there, huh?"

Spencer smiled. "Is your assistant always so keen to look out for your honor?"

"Always."

"Well," he said as he stood and walked over to the door to let Zoe in.

"After you're finished holding court, I'm taking you home, tucking you in, feeding you, and then you and I are going to talk. All night, if necessary, until we get this sorted out." He paused before opening the door. "In case you hadn't noticed," he said with a sly grin, "I'm used to getting my own way, Miss Fairchild."

"And in case *you* hadn't noticed, Mr. Lockhart," Brianna calmly replied as she slipped her shoes back on. "Your strong arm tactics don't work very well with me."

An indignant grunt was Spencer's only reply as he let a wide-eyed Zoe into the room.

Spencer shooed Brianna off to climb into bed, then removed his coat and tie, rolling up his sleeves as he perused her kitchen. It wasn't exactly overflowing with goodies, but there was enough. And, of course, he thought with a smile as he collected assorted utensils and condiments, everything was so logically placed that he could put his hand on anything he needed almost without looking. Twenty minutes later he carried a bed tray with a cheese-and-herb omelette, bagel with cream cheese and jelly, and a large glass of milk into her bedroom.

"You play the part of the invalid very well," he said with a smile as he settled the tray across her lap, resisting the urge to kiss the top of her head.

"I'm hardly an invalid. Although I must admit you're making it look very attractive at the moment." She spread out a linen napkin over her middle and grinned. "This looks wonderful." After the first bite, she added, "It *is* wonderful. You cook?"

Spencer sank into the armchair in the corner and crossed his ankle at his knee. "Almost every night, believe it or not. Mother insisted I learn. I may have grown up with servants, but they never waited on me."

Brianna cocked one eyebrow at him as she chewed. "No spoiled little rich boy?"

"With *my* mother? Not a chance." He leaned against the cushioned back of the chair and watched her eat as he sipped iced tea. The high-neck, long-sleeve cotton nightgown she wore was chosen deliberately, he was certain, for its unalluring qualities. Or so she probably thought. Spencer smiled to himself, studying the row of pearl buttons from her throat to her waist that hinted at the small, high breasts underneath whose silhouettes were just barely visible through the fine fabric. Soft lace edged the collar and cuffs, framing her stubborn jaw and delicate hands with a touch of extra femininity that stirred every nerve ending in his body. She had taken down her hair from its French twist so that it formed a golden cloud around her face and shoulders, setting off those gorgeous sagey eyes even more, which now regarded him with a mixture of amusement and curiosity.

"What?" she asked, wiping her mouth with the edge of the napkin, then placing the tray on the other side of the bed.

"Oh...nothing." He got up and nodded. "All finished?"

"Yes, thank you." She leaned back into the pillows with a great sigh as he picked up the tray. "That was a real treat. Thank you."

"Any time."

In the whole fifteen seconds it took to put the tray in the kitchen he missed her. Returning to her room, he hesitated, then sat on the side of her bed and searched her questioning eyes. Then he lifted tentative fingers to caress a cool cheek.

Her wide eyes flitted back and forth for a second as he pulled her into his arms, then closed as he lowered his mouth to hers. The kiss was straightforward, unapologetic. And possessive. Uncompromisingly possessive.

He felt her arms wrap around his back, her soft mouth melt into his as she returned the kiss. Encouraged, he let his finger trace her jawline, her chin, skimmed down her neck and further down, over the row of buttons so efficiently protecting the contents underneath....

She stiffened, then broke the kiss and pushed herself back, tucking her arms against her ribs. Her face had gone nearly the color of her nightgown.

"Whoa, sweetheart..." His voice was barely above a whis-

per as he gently rubbed her upper arms. "I had no intention
of doing anything more than kiss you—"

She gave a desperate shake of her head. "I can't marry you.
I can't...." Her eyes had been closed; now she opened them,
a tear splashing over her lower lashes and tracking down her
cheek.

Now he was worried. Worried, and still perplexed. He
wiped the tear from her cheek with his thumb, then leaned
back onto the bed on his elbow, taking one of her hands in
his. "Let me get this straight. I'm completely in love with
you, I have no further obligation to Charlotte, I don't give a
damn what anyone thinks about our getting married, but you
still can't go along with this."

She refused to meet his eyes, fiddling with the binding on
the sheet with her free hand. "I—I just can't deal with the
stigma of coming up with a baby five months after I'm married."

She was lying. He was sure of it. Whatever was going on
in her head didn't have one blessed thing to do with this baby
or whatever "stigma" she was so sure would taint their marriage.

Spencer shifted on the bed and looked up into her face.
"But you have no problem with having a baby out of wed-
lock?"

With a grimace, she looked away. "You don't have to make
it sound so nineteenth century." And immediately faced him
again, her eyes glimmering with a pride that made him love
her even more. "Ladies have babies on their own quite a bit
these days." Removing her hand from his, she drew up her
knees and hugged them, resting her chin on the apex. "No—I
have no problem with being a single mother."

Spencer studied her face until she blushed. "I'm not buying
this, Brianna. Not for a minute. We both know you're not
making sense." When she didn't reply, he gently stroked her
forearm; she stiffened again.

He removed his hand. Giving her room, as suspicions began

to crystallize in his thought. "Sweetheart," he asked softly, "*what* are you so afraid of?"

"Afraid?" He could hear the catch in her voice and knew he'd hit paydirt. "What would I be afraid of?"

He touched with her only with his gaze. "That's what I want to know."

Now she flushed scarlet and started trembling so badly the bed shook. "I can't...can't..." Her face dropped into her palms and she shook her head.

His words were very quiet. Very careful. "Does...this have something to do with your getting pregnant?"

Her face still buried in her hands, she allowed just one sharp nod in reply.

He gently claimed her hands in his, then took possession of the frightened eyes, as well. "Brianna—I love you. No matter what. Now...will you tell me what this is all about?"

She couldn't stop shaking. She wanted to tell him; she couldn't tell him.

She had to.

"It goes no farther than this room?"

He touched her cheek. "My love, this has nothing to do with anyone but us."

But us. His words had just made them a unit, she thought in wonder, an impenetrable whole that excluded the rest of the world. He had brought her to the precipice, true, but he would also be the one to catch her before she hit bottom.

She took a deep breath and jumped.

"The father's name is Tom Zimmerman." Thinking Spencer might know him, she glanced at him, but he only shrugged. "I met him at one of my weddings. He was the groom's cousin, some hot-shot attorney with a thriving practice in Dallas."

She brought her knees up to her chin again, feeling Spencer's hand caressing her hair as she talked. "I had had a miserable Christmas. I was completely alone, had no one to even share dinner with..."

"Not even Zoe?"

She shook her head. "She had gone to San Fran for the holidays. So, no. Anyway, I became extremely depressed, although I thought I'd pretty much recovered by the end of January. I have no idea why, but for some reason, this particular wedding threw me right back into it." She bit her lip. When she resumed speaking, her own voice sounded strange, almost disembodied.

"On the surface, Tom was charming, and we seemed to hit it off. We went out for dinner after the wedding, and had a great time. He told me he'd been divorced for several years, even showed me pictures of the kids and lamented not being able to see them very often. He stuck around for a week after the wedding, and we saw each other every evening. To give him credit, he never pushed for an affair, although he hinted broadly enough that he'd be amenable." She closed her eyes, her throat so choked she couldn't speak.

"Did you love him?"

She opened her eyes, her heart skittering at the glint of jealousy in his eyes. "No. I was just…flattered." She lay her head on her knees again, needing to gather her thoughts.

"Brianna?"

"Please…don't push. I'm doing the best I can with this. It…hurts…."

"I know, sweetheart." He moved beside her and gathered her into his arms. "I just thought…that it might be better to get it out as quickly as possible."

She spoke in a monotone as she lay against his chest, listening to his heartbeat through his shirt. With each stroke of his hand over her hair, she was able to push out another part of the whole miserable tale. "It was the last night he was to be in town. The evening had been perfect, *he* had been perfect and funny and attentive. I remember I went to the ladies' room at the restaurant and found myself staring at my reflection in the mirror." She sucked in a breath and said on a stream of air, "The reflection of a thirty-three-year-old virgin who wondered if she'd ever have another chance…"

When she didn't continue, Spencer said with just the slightest tease in his voice, "Is this my cue to make a comment?"

Snuggling closer, she said, "Most people would seem to think it was pretty strange for a woman nowadays to make it into her third decade intact, as it were." She sighed. "My mother had always said I was too picky. And the guys I dated usually said worse."

"So…you decided to prove them wrong?"

"Maybe. I don't know."

She felt his lips gently press into her hair before he said, "I just want to let you know before you say anything more that there's a big difference with being picky and being selective."

"Yeah, well…I was real *selective* that night." She clamped shut her eyes, dredging up images that she had wished over and over and *over* again she could just erase from her mind like she could delete a file from her computer. "He…he became someone else the minute his hotel room door closed. The look on his face…" She shook her head. "It was… horrible. And like some sheltered Victorian daughter, I didn't know what to expect, what I was supposed to feel."

Tears welled up as she began to shake uncontrollably. "He…kept t-telling me if I wasn't such a cold… If I weren't so…frigid, I would enjoy what he was doing to me, that he would enjoy it more, too, even if…" She gulped, then her voice was reduced to a whimper. "Even if it was like m-making love to a broomstick. It was no wonder, he said, that I was still a virgin, with a body like mine.…"

She drew in a long, rattling breath as she felt his arms close around her even more tightly. Was he shaking, too? When she felt some control return to her voice, she continued.

"Afterward, as I lay there in his hotel bed with the sheet pulled up around my inadequate breasts, feeling as though someone had put a hot knife between my legs, he *laughed* at me, clearly delighting in telling me that he wasn't divorced at all, that he'd had a fight with his wife and this was his way of exacting his twisted idea of revenge. His hatred and derision had been directed the whole time at her, not at me—''

''But you're the one who's pregnant,'' Spencer interrupted. ''The bastard didn't even use any protection?''

She heard herself laugh, a small, suffocated sound. ''He told me he'd had a vasectomy.''

A soft expletive escaped Spencer's lips. Then he said, ''I'm amazed, actually, that you wanted to keep this baby—''

''The baby's *mine*,'' she replied, a fierceness in her tone that even surprised her. ''The child will never, ever know about its father.''

''Brianna—this baby will have a father.''

''*No!* That man is dead, as far as I or this baby are concerned—''

''I'm not talking about Tom whatever-his-name-is. I'm talking about me.''

''Spencer...''

''No. Now you listen to me.'' He squeezed her shoulders even more firmly. ''What that guy did to you goes beyond reprehensible. That's not love, sweetheart. Hell, it's not even sex.'' He turned her face to his, pushing back her hair. ''Love-making can be passionate, even frantic sometimes. But it must always be sweet, and respectful, and make both people feel as if the world has just floated away.'' His lips brushed hers, as his hand slowly traveled down her arm. She started to look away. ''No, Brianna—look at me.''

The command was soft, but no less importunate for its gentleness. When she allowed her eyes to meet his, she felt, at last, as if she'd come home.

''This *is* me, not some dysfunctional jerk. And I would never dream of treating a woman that way.'' She shivered as she felt his gaze deliberately travel over her body, even though it was completely covered by the nightgown. ''You're so beautiful you take my breath away every time I see you, did you know that?''

She leaned her forehead against his chest and shook her head.

"Well, you are." He lifted her chin with two fingers and kissed her again, softly. "I remember thinking what an extraordinary creature you were the first time I saw you." With a sigh, he cupped her face in his hand, stroking his thumb across her cheek. "I cherish you as I've never cherished anyone in my life. And, when it's right, I will consider it an honor to make love to you, to show you how wonderful you are. But not tonight. You're in no condition for that right now, either physically or mentally." He paused. "Brianna?"

"Yes?"

"Do you trust me?"

His eyes were frosted fire, soothing and warming simultaneously. "Yes."

"Then...if I can convince you that, together, we can work out your fears, will you reconsider marrying me?"

She already knew the answer to that. Had for some minutes. But sometimes, she decided, there were advantages to not laying all your cards on the table too soon. Maybe Mrs. Franklin was right—maybe she *would* make a helluva poker player.

"I'll...reconsider," she said, and could have cried at the joy she saw in his eyes.

He ran his hand through her hair, his fingers occasionally grazing the lace at the top of her collar. "Do you remember," he asked, his voice low and comforting, "when I asked you if you loved me?"

She nodded, unable to unlock her gaze from his.

"And what did you say?"

"With all my heart," she whispered.

"Then everything else will fall into place." He drew her down into the pillows, cradling her against his chest, stroking her hair and kissing her forehead. She became drowsy, listening to Spencer's endearments, his words of love and kindness and support, and felt, at first, her muscles yield to his ministrations, become relaxed and trusting. When he brought her lips to his, she accepted his kiss with complete abandonment.

Her lips parted willingly to receive his tongue, so gently exploring her mouth, his arms carefully enfolding her as if he were afraid she'd break. He broke the kiss and explored her eyes, his eyebrows quirked in question.

"So far, so good," she said with a little laugh as a quiver run up her spine.

He kissed her again, with a tender passion that ignited a shower of sparks through her whole body. She tensed again, not with apprehension, but with anticipation, with joy and wonder and breathless excitement. When he tentatively skimmed the buttons on her nightgown, she murmured her assent in his ear. His eyes never left hers as one after the other the tiny buttons yielded to his deft fingers, until the front of her nightgown lay open. Only then did his gaze flicker down in a lingering appraisal that brought a flush to her skin.

"Just as I thought," he whispered, once again focusing on her face. "Perfect. And far from inadequate." And then he pulled the nightgown closed over her breasts, redoing the buttons he'd just undone not thirty seconds before. He kissed her again, then searched her face. "Are you still afraid?"

She shook her head, her breathing ragged. Then smiled for him.

He laughed, a sound of nervous relief, and she realized she hadn't been the only one with fears in the room. "Somehow," he said, his voice choked in her ear as he pulled her closer, "I didn't think that would take too long."

A mock cry of indignation flew from her lips as she wrenched herself out of his arms and sat up, then started to swat him with a small ornamental pillow that had gotten knocked to the foot of the bed. "Why, you arrogant, presumptuous..."

Laughing, he stopped her frenzied beating with a hand on her wrist and pulled her down on top of him, and she thought how much she loved his laugh.

How much she loved him.

"So..." he teased, one finger tracing her jaw, "have you reconsidered?"

"Yes," she said softly.

"And?"

"*Yes.*"

He reared back and searched her face.

"Really?"

"Really."

"When?"

She laughed. "There's not much point in waiting, is there?"

He rolled her over and kissed her with such tantalizing sweetness she thought she'd faint. When she opened her eyes, a small burgundy velvet pouch dangled a few inches over her face.

"Well, *take* it," he said, pulling her hand toward him and dropping the little sack into her palm.

She took the pouch from him and sat up, slowly undid the satin drawstring, then spilled out the contents into her hand.

"Oh, Spencer...it's *gorgeous,*" she said on a breath, then squinted at him. "How..."

He finished her thought. "I've been carrying it around since I got back from Japan, transferring it from pocket to pocket, just in case."

She smiled and shook her head. "Just in case, my foot. What am I going to do with you?"

"After we're married, anything you like."

"Very funny." She leaned over and grazed her lips against his, sucking in her breath when he then brought his hand up behind her neck and pulled her mouth to his more tightly. After he released her, she pulled herself upright again, then turned the ring over in her hand, idly wondering what her blood pressure was like at the moment. "It's very old, isn't it?"

"It belonged to my great-grandmother." He grinned. "Mother took it out of the safe two weeks ago and just handed it to me. I didn't have to ask why. She's been rooting for us all along, you know." With a laugh, he said, "Well, silly— put it on. Engagement rings are meant to be worn, not studied."

As he spoke, he took the delicate sapphire ring from her, then slipped it onto her finger. Awestruck, she held it up and shook her head. The round-cut stone, at least a half inch in diameter, was surrounded by small diamonds and tiny seed pearls, all tucked into a gold filigree setting. She giggled. "Gee, if I had known this was part of the deal, I might have said yes a lot sooner—oh!" Then, *"Oh!"*

"What?" Spencer jumped at her exclamation, holding out his hands on either side of her as if she might topple over. "What is it?"

"Well, I'm not sure, but...there! Oh, it is!" Smiling broadly, she took his hand and put it on her middle. "The baby moved, Spence. I just felt my baby move for the first time."

His hand still on her tummy, he nuzzled her neck, turning her into one large goose bump. "No, you didn't, sweetheart."

"Oh, yes, I did, Spence, I'm sure of it. Just keep your hand there a little longer..."

"No, that's not what I meant," he said softly. "You didn't just feel *your* baby move for the first time, my love. You felt *ours.*"

Epilogue

"Good morning, lazybones."

Brianna stirred under the comforter, then stretched and yawned. "Not me. I was up a little earlier."

"Oh? Where was I?"

"Asleep. That's why I came back to bed." She yawned again. "What time is it?" she mumbled.

"After nine."

Grinning, she pulled herself upright, clutching the bedclothes to her collarbone as she tried to focus on Spencer, standing at the foot of the bed holding a bed tray. She loved seeing him slightly disheveled like this, his robe so loosely sashed around his waist that most of his chest was visible, his soft silver hair draped haphazardly over one side of his forehead. With a slow smile, she said, "You're spoiling me, you know."

"It's Sunday morning," he replied as he nestled the bed tray over her thighs. "Besides, after last night, it's the least I can do." He nipped softly at her lower lip, then stood.

A flush washed over her bare skin, and she heard her husband's low laugh.

"I love it when you do that."

"What?"

"Blush. We've been married almost two years, but it's still as if every time is the first." He skimmed a knuckle across her jaw, then down the side of her neck and out over her shoulder. "It's very endearing."

Shivering at his touch, she slanted a look at him from under her eyelashes and gave him a crooked smile. Still holding up the sheet to her breasts, she gestured toward her robe draped across a petit point armchair on the other side of the room. "Just hand me my robe, please, Mr. Lockhart. And is that the paper?" she added, craning her neck to see the chest at the foot of the bed.

"Demanding this morning, aren't we?" Spencer replied with a chuckle as he tossed her the robe, then plopped the paper on the bed beside her while she shimmied into the wisp of ivory charmeuse.

"Where's Melissa?" Brianna asked, carefully working a serrated-edged spoon into a grapefruit half.

"My mother has absconded with her granddaughter to heaven-knows-where. Said they'd see us for lunch. So..." He slowly lowered himself onto the edge of the bed so as to not rock the tray. "The morning's ours. What would you like to do?" The twinkle in those cobalt eyes was unmistakable.

"As if I didn't know what your first choice would be." She eschewed the coffee on the tray and took a sip of orange juice instead, feeling a devilish smile hug at her lips. "You really don't have to keep proving...*things* to me, you know. I get the idea."

His brows dipped slightly. "Getting bored?"

"Ask me again in about fifty years." Then she giggled. "You actually look relieved."

"That's impatience, woman. Are you finished breakfast yet?"

"Just keep your shirt on, buddy," she said, waving a piece of toast in the air. "Or in this case, your robe."

A slight moan escaped Spencer's throat, then he wiggled her foot through the covers. "By the way, Zoe left a message on the machine. Something about bringing in the sketch for Heather Franklin's gown on Tuesday?"

"Oh, right. I'll have to work on it tomorrow, I guess."

As she ate, her thoughts wandered. She had given Zoe her promised promotion after her graduation, and the young woman now managed the business as efficiently as Brianna ever had, as well as lived in her old apartment over the salon. Although Brianna no longer personally attended weddings except as a guest, she still designed the occasional custom ensemble, and had been giving thought to perhaps manufacturing her own line of gowns. Some day.

Sometimes Brianna missed her wonderful apartment and the crazy brides and even the silence in the evenings. But not very often, and not for long.

She loved living in the house in Buckhead, loved having Edwina for company when Spencer had to be away on business. Her fears about Spencer's friends snubbing her had been unfounded. The few who had given him the cold shoulder were not worth bothering about, at least so he said; by and large, his family's friends were like the Lockharts, down-to-earth and more than relieved that he had not married Charlotte after all. And they all seemed to accept little Melissa's appearance with genuine good wishes and excitement and more gifts than one baby could possibly use. Brianna smiled.

Could her life be any better? They had the most beautiful daughter, who resembled a miniature Brianna with her green eyes and golden hair. And every day Brianna thanked her lucky stars for the man she now shared her life with, whose every smile told her how much he loved her, whose every caress told her how much he worshiped her body. And soon…

"Brianna?"

Startled, Brianna turned to the sound of Spencer's low voice on her right. She'd been so lost in her thoughts she hadn't noticed that he'd gotten back into bed.

"Do you ever regret not having a big wedding?"

"Now where on earth did that thought come from?" she asked with a laugh.

"I don't know. Sometimes, though, I wonder if you felt you got gypped. All those extravaganzas you did for everyone else…"

"Which is why I was just as happy with what we did." Another blush rode up her neck as she thought of their hurried nuptials a few days after she finally accepted his proposal, with only his mother, Kelly, Colin, and Zoe in attendance. She touched his cheek, noting that he'd already shaved. "I found it very romantic, sir. And very exciting." She touched her forehead to his. "If you recall."

With a groan, he skimmed his finger over her shoulder, playing with the folds in the charmeuse, then slipped the collar down and brushed his lips over her skin.

"In a minute," she teased, pulling her robe back up over her shoulder. She twisted around and set the bed tray on the floor beside her, then opened the paper and idly flipped through the sections, shivering when he nuzzled her neck. "Stop that!" she giggled as she felt his hand begin to caress her thigh. "Oh, look at this, would you?" She tossed Spencer the society pages and leaned back against the pillows.

Spencer pulled a pair of reading glasses off the nightstand, then lay back on his pillow, peering through them at the article and photo she pointed out to him. He gave a low chuckle. "I hope she likes this photo better than she liked the last one."

"Well," Brianna said, leaning the side of her face in her hand, "if she doesn't, at least her husband-to-be is a plastic surgeon."

Spencer removed the glasses, snapped the paper to his chest and seemed to scrutinize the ceiling for a moment, then rolled his head toward her on his pillow. "I really hope Charlotte will be happy," he said quietly.

Brianna smiled and traced his collarbone with her finger. "I know you do. So do I, actually."

Spencer tossed the paper onto the floor and lunged at her, scooping her into his arms, sending her into peals of laughter. "Good God, I love you, woman!" he said, burying his face in her neck.

"Spencer?" she managed to say between gasps.

"Hmm?" came the muffled response from under her earlobe.

"Remember Christmas? At the Connecticut house with Kelly and Colin and baby Edwin?"

Resting his cheek on her shoulder, he offered her a wicked grin. "Oh, I remember. Vividly." He pulled down the collar of her robe again in order to let his lips linger on the little bone at the very top of her arm, then undid the sash of her robe. "Best damn Christmas I've ever had, I tell you."

"Well, it appears we're going to have a little souvenir from that trip." She took his hand and slipped it underneath her robe, onto her bare abdomen. "While you were snoozing so peacefully this morning, I was taking a pregnancy test." Then she just smiled.

"You little turkey!" He pushed himself up on one elbow. "Why didn't you wake me up?"

"I just wanted a few minutes to savor it by myself, that's all."

He kissed the top of her head and nodded, then pulled her to him.

"And...you don't mind having another baby so soon after Melissa?"

"Are you kidding?" She skated her fingers over his chest and sighed. "It's the only time I have breasts."

He laughed and squeezed her shoulder. They lay still for a long moment, suspended in time, and then she felt the pressure of his warm hand increase, just slightly, on her tummy, still soft from little Melissa's birth. As his fingers flicked across her navel in a tantalizing caress, she asked, "I take it you're pleased?"

Her heart melted at the expression of wonder dancing across his face.

"Pleased?" He touched her lips and locked her into those kind, loving eyes. Into his soul. "I'm absolutely delighted."

Then he slipped his hand behind her head and brought her mouth up to his.

* * * * *

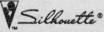

Take 4 bestselling love stories FREE

Plus get a FREE surprise gift!

Special Limited-time Offer

Mail to Silhouette Reader Service™

3010 Walden Avenue
P.O. Box 1867
Buffalo, N.Y. 14269-1867

YES! Please send me 4 free Silhouette Yours Truly™ novels and my free surprise gift. Then send me 4 brand-new novels every other month, which I will receive months before they appear in bookstores. Bill me at the low price of $2.90 each plus 25¢ delivery and applicable sales tax, if any.* That's the complete price and a savings of over 10% off the cover prices—quite a bargain! I understand that accepting the books and gift places me under no obligation ever to buy any books. I can always return a shipment and cancel at any time. Even if I never buy another book from Silhouette, the 4 free books and the surprise gift are mine to keep forever.

201 SEN CF2X

Name	(PLEASE PRINT)	
Address	Apt. No.	
City	State	Zip

This offer is limited to one order per household and not valid to present Silhouette Yours Truly™ subscribers. *Terms and prices are subject to change without notice. Sales tax applicable in N.Y.

USYRT-296

©1996 Harlequin Enterprises Limit

ALICIA SCOTT

Continues the
twelve-book series—
36 Hours—in March 1998
with Book Nine

PARTNERS IN CRIME

The storm was over, and Detective Jack Stryker finally had a prime suspect in Grand Springs' high-profile murder case. But beautiful Josie Reynolds wasn't about to admit to the crime— nor did Jack want her to. He believed in her innocence, and he teamed up with the alluring suspect to prove it. But was he playing it by the book—or merely blinded by love?

For Jack and Josie and *all* the residents of Grand Springs, Colorado, the storm-induced blackout was just the beginning of 36 Hours that changed *everything!* You won't want to miss a single book.

Available at your favorite retail outlet.

Silhouette ®

TM

Welcome to *Love Inspired*™

A brand-new series of contemporary inspirational love stories.

Join men and women as they learn valuable lessons about facing the challenges of today's world and about life, love and faith.

Look for the following March 1998 Love Inspired™ titles:

CHILD OF HER HEART
by Irene Brand

A FATHER'S LOVE
by Cheryl Wolverton

WITH BABY IN MIND
by Arlene James

Available in retail outlets in February 1998.

LIFT YOUR SPIRITS AND GLADDEN YOUR HEART
with *Love Inspired!*™

Steeple Hill™

LI398